It had been ten years, but he still thought of her often.

Ten years, and the mere sight of a woman who resembled Miranda Tyler ruined Dr. Caleb Blackfox's day. He'd saved hundreds of lives, healed the sick, donated thousands to charity and confessed his sins at church. Yet he didn't think he'd ever earn Miranda's forgiveness.

But he could never stop thinking about her. She had the kind of body that could stop a man in his tracks. It had never failed to amaze Caleb that Miranda never noticed her effect on the men around her. He'd loved that about her—her intensity, her focus. They would walk into a room, and he knew that all his friends were staring at the amazing girl he had on his arm. But she didn't even notice....

Ten years before, she'd said that she never wanted to see him again. And so Caleb would not approach her now. But no matter how hard he tried to put her out of his mind, he couldn't help wondering when she had come back home, and what she was doing in his hospital.

Books by Angela Weaver

Kimani Romance

A Love to Remember
The Very Thought of You

Kimani Arabesque

By Design
By Intent
Blind Obsession
Taking Chances

ANGELA WEAVER

is a Southern girl by way of Tennessee. She's lived in Philadelphia, Atlanta, Washington, D.C., New York and Tokyo, Japan. An avid reader and occasional romantic optimist, she began writing her first novel on a dare, and hasn't stopped since. Having heeded the call to come home to the South, she has returned to Atlanta. On weekends she can be found hiking in the north Georgia mountains, scuba diving or working on her next book.

THE
VERY
THOUGHT
of
YOU

ANGELA WEAVER

KIMANI
ROMANCE

This one is for you, Tarb.

I owe you for restoring my belief that the
human heart is neither fickle nor unkind.

I thank you for being my breakfast buddy.

I appreciate you for being an inspiration and showing
me that there are people in this world who love fiercely
and are not afraid to show it.

I am blessed to be your friend.

 KIMANI PRESS™

ISBN-13: 978-0-373-86026-5
ISBN-10: 0-373-86026-9

THE VERY THOUGHT OF YOU

www.kimanipress.com

Printed in U.S.A.

Dear Reader,

Many of you have asked about Caleb, and I hope you've enjoyed reading about the handsome doctor as much as I've had fun writing about him. I'm looking forward to bringing you more tales of the Blackfox clan, and appreciate all your e-mails and support.

Please feel free to send me a note at angela@angelaweaver.com or visit me on the Web at www.angelaweaver.com.

sMiLes,

Angela

Chapter 1

Rome, the center of the universe a thousand years ago in Italy, had a cousin in Georgia. *No, more like little sister,* Miranda thought wryly, as she stepped out of the rental car. Since she'd left home, the city had almost doubled in population, thanks to Atlanta's increasing popularity. She'd only been home for less than three hours, but already she could see the changes. There were new street signs, parks, shopping plazas and traffic lights. She never would have thought that some day the town would boast a tourism industry. No matter the new additions, the things she loved about her hometown still remained the same. The slow pace, the family-owned shops, the way people smiled, the fresh air, high hills and abundant trees.

If you asked anyone who knew her, they would say that Miranda could never live in a small town. But wouldn't they be shocked at how easy it would be for her to give up Washington, D.C.'s fast pace and fall back into the relaxed Southern lifestyle. If anyone had told her that she would be taking a leave of absence and returning home with a child in tow, she would have thought them insane. She didn't avoid coming home, but she dreaded it. Not because of family, but because of memories. Memories of the best and the worst times of her life. Memories of the man who'd put her over the moon with joy, and then broke her heart into so many pieces she still didn't know if she had it all together.

She'd dated more than her share of highly prized metro D.C. area's eligible bachelors, and had even managed to be the recipient of two marriage proposals. Miranda's brow creased at the thought of why she hadn't said yes. The men were as close to her "wish list" for a mate as possible. Only when she'd sat up all night and finished a bottle of wine with her girlfriends did she realize why she couldn't accept their proposals. No matter how much she'd wanted to ignore it, the truth was that she'd never felt the passion, the connection, the soul-deep commitment that had existed between her and Caleb Blackfox.

A rush of annoyance tore into her. After all these years, he still had a hold on her heart. He was the main reason she'd avoided coming home. But here she was, with three suitcases in the trunk of her rental car, about to walk into Mercy Hospital. Miranda exhaled slowly, trying, and partially succeeding, to calm the flutter in the pit of her stomach. Instead of thinking about the past, she concentrated on the present situation.

She'd needed a vacation; that wasn't a problem. If she had woken up one morning and decided to cash in all of her paid time off, she wouldn't have to set foot in the office for at least six months. While working for the U.S. Marshals Service for the past five years had been a boon for her career, it had left her with little personal time. And now, even though she was officially on leave to take care of a family matter, she'd brought her work with her.

Opening up the back door of her rental car, Miranda pulled out a shopping bag with a few things she'd purchased for Darren before leaving D.C.

"Ms. Miranda?"

"Call me Mom or Mommy, Kelly," Miranda corrected. The door closed and an eleven-year-old girl stood neatly dressed in blue jeans, jacket and tennis shoes, and was clutching an oversize book bag.

Ebony black ponytails tied with red ribbons sprouted from both sides of her head. It had taken Kelly over twenty minutes to create the perfect part and another twenty minutes to get dressed. Now the perfectly coordinated little girl looked up at Miranda with solemn light brown eyes. *Ryan's eyes,* Miranda remembered and wondered why she'd never noticed. Maybe it was the fact that the little girl more resembled the mother Miranda had never had the chance to meet.

Kelly sighed. "*Mom,* is your brother nice?"

Miranda reached down and took the little girl's hand as they crossed the parking lot in the direction of the hospital's main entrance. Was Darren nice? She briefly cataloged a list of her older brother's personality traits and rapidly came to the conclusion that *nice* would not be an adjective to describe Darren Tyler. "Umm, he's loyal, a little overprotective and loves dogs," she added.

"Did you know that Daddy said that when he comes back he's going to get me a puppy?"

Miranda nodded and looked both ways for the third time before crossing. She was cautious by nature, but ever since Kelly had come into her life she'd gone to the extreme. When they'd stopped at various shopping malls on the drive down, she hadn't let Kelly out of her sight—

even going so far as to stand guard outside of the dressing room. "I think he mentioned it before."

The child smiled so widely that Miranda got a bird's-eye view of the metal braces in her mouth. "Good. That way I can remind him, just in case he tries to get out of it."

"That's the last thing he would ever do, baby cakes," Miranda responded, using Ryan's pet name for his daughter. Her mind hummed with an added task. Depending on the length of time they stayed in the town she would have to find Kelly an orthodontist. Not to mention a pediatrician, a dentist and an after-school tutor. Wherever the agency decided to place Ryan and Kelly after the trial, she would make sure that the little girl remained an A student.

Her steps slowed as they moved toward the gently curving glass curtain wall that formed the lobby at the main entrance. Her mother had mentioned in passing during one of their weekend conversations the previous year that the new hospital was high-tech and now she truly believed her. She would have expected to come across this type of building in Washington, D.C., not in her hometown. But they had outdone themselves with a striking lobby of glass and brick. Tall light fixtures that could have doubled as works of art filled the lobby with a rainbow of soft colors from the sun's rays.

She walked through the second set of the hospital's automatic doors. Outwardly everything about Miranda stayed the same. Inwardly, however, she shivered. Darren's automobile accident brought home the fact that life was pretty fragile, and with their parents out of the country, volunteering in Africa, he was pretty much the only family she could depend on.

Miranda felt a tug on her hand and turned to look at Kelly with a raised brow. "Mir—" she started then stopped. "Mommy, I don't like hospitals."

"Me, either," she responded truthfully. Miranda's heart went out to the child. Although she'd never experienced the death of a parent, she provided support for enough friends and colleagues who had lost loved ones to know how badly it hurt. Kelly's mother had died over a year ago, and both the child and her father had yet to heal. "I promise that we won't stay long. I know you're probably a little tired from the drive and I could use a shower. Do you think you can hang with me a little while longer?"

"No problem." Kelly nodded.

Miranda smiled with gratitude. At first when her boss and Ryan had come to her with the idea of bringing Kelly with her to Georgia, she'd been vehemently opposed to the plan. Now, as she approached the front desk, she was truly grateful for the small hand she held.

"Hello, we're here to see Darren Tyler."

"He's in the ICU, miss. Visitors are limited to family only." The voice was impatient and bored.

Narrowing her eyes, Miranda looked down and across the woman's shirt to locate her identification badge. "Mrs. Walters, we *are* his family," she said coldly. "I'm his little sister."

The woman looked at Miranda closely. For a moment she thought she would have to pull out her driver's license to prove who she was. Had the situation not been so urgent, she would have taken the receptionist to task for her rude behavior. After a moment, the lady on the other side of the desk returned her gaze to the computer.

"He's on the fifth floor. Room 503," she said.

"Thank you," Miranda replied curtly before turning on her heel and stomping away with Kelly at her side. Swallowing, Miranda moved toward the elevators. While waiting for the car, and trying to calm herself down by focusing on trivial things, she noticed that the furnishings were warm and natural tones grouped in small clusters, more like an intimate hotel, and completely devoid of any hint of the white sterile environment often associated with hospitals.

"Are you going to be all right?"

She blinked and looked down into Kelly's worried brown eyes. Here she was, a grown woman being comforted by a child. It was almost funny if it wasn't so humiliating. Forcing a smile to her face she nodded. "Right as rain."

They took the elevator up and, by navigating the many signs, she soon found her brother's room. Holding Kelly's small hand in hers and the shopping bag in the other, she entered the hospital room.

An hour later, life hadn't gotten any better.

"Miranda Tyler doesn't cry," she muttered under her breath as she stepped through the glass doorway of her brother's hospital room. No tears at funerals, sniffles while watching old black-and-white movies, or choked sobs after hearing the verdict in a murder case. None. She took another deep breath and gripped the two soda cans in her hands. The cold had almost numbed her fingers, but she didn't want to let them go. It was easier to concentrate on the uncomfortable pain in her fingertips than to think about how close her brother had come to death.

Swallowing back the sob stuck in her throat, she crossed the small room to the couch, leaned down and tapped Kelly on the shoulder. It took the little girl a moment to glance up from her laptop and slip back one of the earphones.

"I thought you could use something to drink," she said holding up both soda cans. Catching Kelly's confused glance, Miranda shrugged. "I forgot to ask what kind you liked to drink, so I purchased the most popular choice among kids of your age group."

Kelly shook her head and smiled up at Miranda. "You think way too much, Ms. Tyler. Anything's okay with me."

Relieved, Miranda handed over one of the sodas, opened the other one and took a drink. She should have corrected Kelly, but she didn't have the heart. In the past she'd always been one of the people instructing new arrivals on the process of getting into the Witness Protection Agency. It was the administrative work she was most familiar with. She'd never had to get close, never had to witness someone lose their very identity. Nor did she think that she would ever be on assignment and have to be a participant in the act. The carbonated liquid stung her throat and made her eyes water. Almost like tears, almost like she was crying. Wiping them away quickly, she turned back to the man lying in the hospital bed.

"Is he going to be okay?" Kelly asked.

Miranda turned her attention to Kelly, pasted a small smile on her face and prayed she at least sounded more convincing than she felt. "The doctors said he'd be okay."

"Do you believe them?"

She flashed back to the meeting she'd had with Darren's treating physician. Physically, her brother was slated to make a full recovery, but they couldn't completely rule out the possible long-term effects of a head injury. "Darren doesn't have a choice. He's going to come out of this."

"Just like my dad, right?" Kelly asked.

Miranda nodded and a smile tickled her lips as she thought of Ryan. She'd known from the moment she'd first stepped into the room with the Federal Marshal that nothing would keep that man from what was his. That sentiment was doubled where his family was concerned. "Oh, yes. If you'll just bear with me for another hour, we'll go back to the hotel, grab some room service and you can get some sleep."

Taking two steps toward the bed, Miranda wished she could call her parents, but there was nothing they could do because they were so far away. She calculated it would take at least a week for them to make arrangements to return from Ghana. Not to mention, teaching in the stable African country had given her parents a new lease on life and a second wind to a stagnant marriage.

She looked down into Darren's face, so like her father's, and sniffed as her heartbeat stuttered. Same wide forehead, stubborn jaw and thick head of hair. Her larger than life, personal hero, older brother was hooked up to a machine and had his leg in traction. That dose of reality almost brought

Miranda to her knees. She reached out and clutched the bed's side railing for balance as she repeated another mantra.

"Miranda Tyler does not panic," she whispered.

"No, you don't, little sister," a raspy voice replied.

She blinked and looked down into Darren's bloodshot brown eyes. "You're awake!"

He grimaced and his tongue moved over his cracked lips. "Thirsty."

Quickly Miranda moved to the bedside table, poured a glass of water and held it to his lips. Darren took a couple of sips and settled back.

"How are you feeling?"

"Like someone took a baseball bat and beat me like a piñata." He grimaced and took a few deep breaths. "What happened?"

"You don't remember?" Miranda asked as she took his hand and gently squeezed.

"I remember driving home from the office and thinking about what I was going to eat while watching Georgia beat the hell out of Auburn. After that, everything gets fuzzy. I recall a woman screaming and an ambulance. That's all I know before waking up and seeing you talking to yourself."

"That was approximately forty-eight hours ago."

His eyebrows shot up and then he winced. "What!"

"Yes." Miranda nodded. "You've been unconscious for the past two days, big brother. Guess you should have driven a little more carefully."

His brow furrowed and Miranda could see his mind kick into the next gear. "Wait a minute. Wait a minute. How the hell could I have driven more carefully? That damn Lincoln hit me."

Miranda smiled widely. A real smile. A smile that reached down to the tips of her toes. Just hearing Darren curse let her know things were looking up. Plus there was the bonus that his memory of the accident was returning.

"If you'd been on top of your game, you would have been able to dodge the seventy-two-year-old man who accidentally swerved into your lane as he was reaching for his cell phone."

"Yeah, right," he replied. "What are you doing here? Who called you?"

"Uncle Ron called me before he had to go out of town."

"Miranda, you need to get on that phone of yours and book a ticket back to D.C. I'm fine."

Miranda leaned forward and narrowed her eyes at her older brother, her closest friend and the one man other than her father she'd never in her life doubted. From what she'd read in the newspaper and gleaned from the accident reports, if he had been driving his small sports car instead of his SUV, he wouldn't be alive. "You have a concussion, two fractured ribs, sprained wrist, and fracture in your right ankle and a broken leg."

"So? I can still take care of myself. You have a life and a job that you need to get back to."

She pursed her lips. "You know damn well that my life is my job. But that's irrelevant. Let me put the situation in simple terms. You had a car accident, I took vacation. That's a perfect match. Now suck it up and deal with it. For the first time in our lives, this little sister is going to take care of her older brother."

"Miranda..."

She cut him off. "If it makes you feel better, I had to leave D.C. anyway."

"Guy problems?"

She shook her head. "No."

"Are you in danger?" he asked.

Miranda shook her head. "No, we just needed to get away for a little while."

As a project specialist within the Justice Department, she worked directly for the Witness Protection Agency. Her job was to assist in the relocation and protection of those within the system. Miranda worked behind the scenes to manage logistics, work through the internal bureaucracy and make sure agents in the field had every possible resource to perform their abilities, but she'd never gotten involved...until now.

"*We?* Who the hell is we?"

"Me." Kelly's high-pitched voice came out clearly over the hum of the hospital monitoring equipment.

Darren turned his head and aimed a penetrating stare at Kelly. Miranda could see the wheels turning in her brother's head and her stomach dropped a little.

"Miranda, who is she?" Darren asked the question without turning his attention from the girl on the two-seat sofa.

She turned her head to look to Kelly and caught the flicker of amusement in Kelly's somber brown eyes. *Good Lord,* Miranda thought, *the girl deserves an Academy Award.*

Miranda drew in a deep breath and let it out slowly. "Darren, meet Kelly." She paused, then said with a wink, "She's my daughter."

Chapter 2

"I'm not taking sides," Caleb Blackfox repeated for the third time in the last half hour. He rubbed his eyes and sighed. He took a drag of his coffee and looked around. Even after the million-dollar renovation of the hospital, no matter how many plants, how much music and bright color, the hospital cafeteria was still a cafeteria. What kind of drama would have his cousin sitting here now? Nothing could make a man turn backflips more than his little sister. Caleb closed his eyes and let out a mental prayer.

Thank God his own little sister, Regan, had finally gotten married. Caleb didn't have a gray hair on his head but everybody had predicted that all the men in their family would have their hair falling out because of his only sister. After spending years traipsing around the world for the state department, she'd settled into working on domestic assignments.

His cousin Kevin wiped the cinnamon-roll crumbs from his mouth and sat forward. "Look, she listens to you."

"The hell she does. If Savannah had listened to me, she wouldn't be about to elope with Archer."

"You talked to her?"

"She asked me to recommend an obstetrician," he said flatly.

"And you did?"

"What choice do I have? Yeah, I'm not happy that she's about to marry the great-grandson of the man who almost destroyed our family. Yeah, I think she was wrong to hide the relationship from her family. But, what's done is done and medically speaking the deed can't be reversed. You might as well get used to being an uncle and calling your sister by the Archer last name."

"The hell I will. I don't care if she marries him. Savannah and that baby will have Blackfox blood in their veins."

"And Archer."

Kevin's jaw clenched. "Damn, you don't have to remind me."

"That baby is either going to help this family heal or tear it apart," Caleb stated.

"At least you can get your head around her marrying the man."

He sighed as weariness seeped deep into his bones. "She loves him. Who are we to stand in the way of that?"

Just the thought sent his mind hurtling to the past. It had been ten years and he'd still thought of her often. Ten years and still the mere sight of a woman who resembled Miranda ruined his day. He'd saved hundreds of lives, healed the sick, donated thousands to charity and confessed all his sins to Deacon James last Easter. Yet he didn't think he'd ever get forgiveness from one woman.

Man, she had a behind that could stop a man in his tracks. It had never failed to amaze Caleb that Miranda never noticed. He'd loved that about her, her intensity, her focus. They would walk into a room and he knew that all of his fraternity brothers were staring at the amazing girl he'd had on his arm, but she wouldn't notice. Some things didn't change. Nothing would have kept him from recognizing his first love in the hospital corridors. Her words—that she never wanted to see him again—had kept Caleb from approaching her. More than anything else he wanted to know when had she come home and why was she at the hospital? Caleb put those questions on hold and attempted to concentrate on his cousin's conversation.

"You'll talk to her, cuz?"

He shook his head. "I'll give her my blessings. She's a grown woman, Kevin."

"She's my little sister."

Caleb finished off his soda. The entire conversation was a reminder of why he avoided family politics. He didn't want to get involved. The only thing that mattered to him at the moment was finding out if the woman he'd seen exiting the elevator was also the first woman he'd ever loved. "I wish you luck, but don't include me in any plans of yours. Thanks for lunch, but I have to get back to work."

Both men stood and after a quick hug, Caleb strode out of the cafeteria, took the stairs to the patient wings and went directly to the closest nurses' workstation.

"Good evening, Dr. Blackfox. Can I help you with something?"

Caleb summoned a smile and stood over the attending nurse. "I just need to use your computer to track down a patient, if that's all right."

"Of course. I have to see to Mrs. Brinkle's medication. Take your time."

As he sat down in the seat and entered Miranda's name, conflicting emotions of dread and excitement filled his mind. What if she was a patient at the hospital? What if she were married? But the excitement of seeing her again turned to disappointment when her name returned no results. Just to make sure he searched by last name.

Darren Tyler—car accident—stable condition—fifth floor.

Relief loosened every muscle in his body. She was okay. Caleb sat back in the seat and stared at the screen. Miranda's brother was in the hospital. At that point, he should have cleared his search and returned to his rounds, but he didn't. Caleb stared at the room number. This could be a sign. He'd spent years in the academic world and he'd been trained to look at facts, examine evidence and make diagnoses based on science. However, a decade of academics could never erase a childhood steeped in rich folklore, Baptist traditions and spiritual learning.

In the Blackfox family, with its African and Native-American roots, when people spoke about their dreams everyone listened. Last week, during last week's family bimonthly Sunday dinner, his grandmother had mentioned that she'd dreamed about deer running along the edge of the lake. The last time she'd had a dream like that his little sister had gone and brought home her future husband, Kincaid.

A month ago, his aunt had dreamed about crabs. Although his colleagues could have chalked it up to midnight cravings, his mother had explained that it meant a long and difficult courtship for lovers. His own parents had puzzled over who in the family that could mean because no one else seemed to be in any kind of relationship. The mystery was solved a few weeks later with Savannah's announcement that she was pregnant. His unmarried cousin had somehow managed to fall in love with not only the last man on earth, but the great-grandson of the man who'd almost singlehandedly destroyed their family.

So that brought him back to his present situation. Miranda Tyler was in town, in his hospital, possibly brought back to his life for a second chance. And here he was, a doctor who spent his life giving his patients a second chance. Didn't he deserve one as well? Caleb stood up, adjusted his coat and headed for the stairs. Knowing Miranda as he did, and appreciating the fact that she probably would have changed very little in the time away, he'd need an edge to get close. Looking down at his badge, his mouth curled up in a grin.

The next morning, Caleb exited the stairwell on the fifth floor and greeted the on-duty nursing staff. "Good morning," he said cheerfully.

Almost happy enough to whistle, he pulled out Darren Tyler's chart and was reviewing it when one of his favorite nurses rounded the corner and maneuvered to take her place at the circular station.

"Never really see you on this floor, Dr. Black-fox. Got a new patient?"

Caleb cocked his head to the side and thought for a second. "Old friend, actually. Darren Tyler."

Peggy's eyes widened. "You know him?"

"I used to date his sister in college."

"You went out with Miranda?"

"What's so incredible about that?"

"She doesn't seem to be your type."

"Why wouldn't she be my type?"

"She's nice and considerate. For example, she brought us a basket of cookies and gift boxes of bath stuff yesterday morning just to say thank you for taking care of her brother."

"What are you saying—that I'm not a nice guy?"

"No. You just don't seem to date real women. I've had the unfortunate luck to meet at least two of your ex-stalkers. Oh, sorry, ex-girlfriends."

"Rhonda was off of her medication that day."

"That woman needs a permanent prescription and an attitude drip. She lost it just because you didn't drop everything to look at her throat."

"As you can see, Miranda isn't like that."

"She's sweet and that brother of hers is some-thing else. If I didn't have that man of mine taking care of business at home, I'd be tempted."

"So Miranda visits in the morning?"

"Yep. The first time she brought that cute little girl of hers. This morning she came by herself."

Caleb's body froze. *Little girl.* The nurse's words repeated in his head. The ache in his heart turned to a full-blown pain worse than any heartburn he'd ever suffered through. Was she married? The thought of her having a family tore his gut. "She has a little girl?"

"Her name's Kelly. Cute as a button, smart as a whip and very well-mannered. And she's a little computer whiz. Little thing showed me how to change the resolution on this monitor, so now I think we all have a better chance of not going blind." Peggy shook her head and then snorted. "Kids these days are surfing the net and sending e-mail before learning how to ride a bike. Pretty frightening if you ask me."

"How old is she?"

Helen frowned. "I think she told me she was ten or eleven years old."

A cold sweat broke out on his brow as his mind did an instant calculation from the last time he and Miranda had been together physically. The answer gave him a chill. Depending on the length of her pregnancy... "Did you say ten years?"

"Yes. Why are you looking like you've seen a ghost?"

"Just surprised. I just didn't know that Miranda had gotten married."

"Well, she didn't have a ring. Kelly didn't talk about her father much, but you could tell she loves her momma."

"Well, if it's okay with you I'm going to check on the patient."

"Be my guest. He just took a dose of meds, so he's probably knocked out."

Caleb stepped into the room and looked down at Darren's sleeping face. Even when the man had his eyes closed he could easily remember the last time they'd spoken. Miranda's older brother's harsh voice echoed in his ears.

"Don't you think you've hurt my sister enough, Blackfox? I always knew you'd show your true colors. You rich people don't care who you hurt as long as you get what you want. Well, you bastard, you can't have my sister. Now get the hell out of this house before I call the cops."

Hate. Miranda may have despised him for his infidelity, but Darren had hated him from the moment he found out that they were dating. No one was good enough for the man's little sister, even a Blackfox.

Caleb stepped aside and moved the blanket and hospital gown. He examined Darren's chest, satisfied that the bruises there were healing. He continued to observe the man's vital signs and looked down at his face. No matter how many times they'd fought, Caleb had always respected Darren. The man had only been looking out for his little sister. He'd done the same thing for his little sister, Regan.

But no matter how much he and his brothers had tried to protect her, she'd still managed to get into trouble. Then Regan had grown up. He shook his head and smiled slightly. His little sister was grown up, married even, and if her new husband had anything to do about it, Caleb would soon have his first niece or nephew to spoil.

"Dr. Blackfox, Miranda Tyler—the patient's sister—was wondering if it was okay to come in."

Caleb lifted his head and swung his gaze around to collide with that of the woman who'd been his first true love.

For a moment they stood frozen as several heartbeats passed; their eyes locked and bodies still. His vision was filled with the image of the last time they'd been together. Before the arguments, before her tears. He saw the sweet smile on her lips as he'd held her in his arms with the sunlight streaming through the open blinds of his downtown condominium.

His fingers gripped the folder and pen in his hands as he remembered the smooth silk of her skin and the soft round curve of her belly. One of his favorite moments was when they'd lie in bed or on the sofa and he would place his hand on her stomach. No matter how stressed out he'd been with school, Miranda would calm him. She'd been his good-luck charm, his peace and his one weakness.

The business outfit she wore, a black pantsuit and gray blouse, made her look more sophisticated, feminine and alluring. Then there were the high-heeled shoes that would bring her closer to his six-foot-three-inch height. He'd loved it when she'd worn her stilettos and he knew just how well she could maneuver with them when they were alone in the bedroom.

A sigh of regret slipped through his lips. Now looking at her, he could see that she'd grown even more beautiful after all the years. His gaze moved to her reddish-brown hair and he couldn't help but notice that she'd let it grow. Parted in the middle, side-swept bangs fell below her jawline, drawing his eyes to her delicate chin and bow-shaped lips. Her face had grown slender with the years, and her cheekbones were more pronounced. His eyes settled there for a moment as his body clenched with the memory of those lips. If he'd ever had a turn-on, Miranda's lips had been the thing, besides his loving her backside. His oldest brother was a leg man. Not him. Caleb inwardly shook his head.

His preferences started at her nice curvaceous

backside, then moved to her mouth and ended
with her eyes. Her eyes. He loved to watch the
play of emotion in Miranda's eyes. She'd had one
of the best poker faces he'd ever seen, but it was
all for naught because he could tell what she was
feeling when he looked into her cinnamon brown
eyes. At that moment they were darker than he'd
ever seen them. And if he could guess, he'd say
she'd been just as effected by his presence as he
was by hers.

Finally, when the silence began to border on
discomfort, he smiled. "Miranda Tyler, as I live
and breathe," Caleb said warmly.

Her brow rose and he glimpsed the slight for-
mation of a smile on her lips. "Dr. Blackfox, what
a surprise."

He maneuvered around the bed. As if it were
the most natural thing for him to do, he swept her
into his arms for a hug. And as her arms wrapped
around his sides, his body relaxed in happiness.
Even after all those years, they still fit together
and she felt damn good. Taking a deep breath,
Caleb reluctantly pulled away; but unwilling to
break the physical connection, he kept his hands
on her arms. Looking down into her upturned
face, he grinned. "We had an agreement before I
even took the first MCAT that you would only call
me *doctor* at a very special time."

Blood suffused her cheeks and she looked away.

A flash of triumph shot through his veins. She hadn't forgotten. They'd known each other since junior high school, but everything changed in college. Back home she'd been the girl next door. All it had taken was the sight of Miranda in a tight skirt to bring him to his knees. Their first date had been a smoldering fire; their first kiss blew his mind. Whenever they'd been in the room together, sparks had flown.

"That was a lifetime ago."

"But the Miranda I knew always kept her promises."

She shook her head and a slight smile curved her lips upward. "I haven't been that girl in a long time, Caleb."

"Well, although I dislike the circumstances, I'm glad you're home. Will you be staying for a while?"

"I'll be here as long as Darren needs me."

"He could have a pretty lengthy recovery," he said in all seriousness. "I'm sure there's someone waiting for you back north who won't be happy to hear that."

She shrugged. "I'm on leave from work. I can be here as long as it takes for him to recover."

His eyes narrowed on her vague reply. As far as he could tell, Miranda had come alone. He'd taken in the lack of a wedding band the moment she'd walked into the room. That observation, coupled with her response, led him to believe that she wasn't married or in a committed relationship. And having met her parents, he knew that if she'd had a child, she would have to have a husband. Unless…

Caleb glanced around. A few of the nurses were milling about in the hallway and seemed particularly interested in what was going on. Without a doubt, all the hospital staff from the chief to the orderlies would know about the hug by the end of the day. The line between personal and private had been drawn long ago.

Caleb made a point to look at his watch. "I'm due to go on a required break and was headed down to the cafeteria. Care to join me? We could catch up. The last I heard you were in New York."

She shook her head. "I spent a few weeks there for training, but I live in D.C. now."

"Nice. I look forward to hearing about what you've been up to for the past couple of years."

"I'm not so sure that would be a good idea."

Not wanting to lose the opportunity to question her about the little girl, Caleb quickly added, "I don't bite and I don't carry needles. If you don't want to talk about your personal life, then we can discuss your brother's condition."

"Of course. I could use a cup of coffee."

Caleb stood close to her in the elevator, and to Miranda's surprise, heat trickled up and down her body. Miranda wanted to scream in frustration. It had taken her *years* not months to get Caleb Blackfox out of her system. Why in the world would she have a reaction to him now?

Because I am an idiot, she told herself. It had to be. Coming back to Rome was taking a leap back in time, and she'd forgotten to bring an anti-idiocy jacket with her.

"I'm sure that this was an unexpected inconvenience," he mentioned. "I would have expected your parents to be here."

Miranda kept her eyes on direction markers in the hallway. There were signs for the emergency room, women's wing, restrooms, surgery and finally the cafeteria. It came as second nature for her to observe and memorize her surroundings. And that training came in handy as a distraction from the man at her side. She'd never really been in a hospital. Lucky for her no one in her family had needed a visit.

"Are your parents well?"

Caleb's question pulled Miranda from her thoughts. She turned her head to look at him. "They're teaching high school in Ghana."

"For how long?"

"It was supposed to be a year. The last time I spoke with them things were going so well that they may decide to sign on for another year."

"How do you feel about that? I know you were very close to your parents."

His question, although innocent, sparked tears in her eyes. Quickly looking away, Miranda blinked rapidly. It was utterly selfish, but she wanted them home; she wanted her father to be there to tell her everything was going to be okay while her mother hugged her tight. Although she could depend on her aunt Francine to help out, her father's sister had her own household to deal with. Just as she almost gave in to a self-pity session, she found herself pulled into a man's chest.

"It's going to be okay," he soothed.

For a moment she fought against his embrace, but it was all but impossible. No matter how much mental distance Miranda had been able to put between her and Caleb, her body still reacted to the scent of his cologne, the hard contours of his body and the strength of his arms.

She drew in a deep breath and opened her eyes. A blush roared into her cheeks. Every eye on the floor seemed to be watching their little show. Pulling back, Miranda pasted a smile on her face. "Thank you."

"I'm here for you anytime you need me," Caleb replied. "Now how about that cup of coffee?"

A few minutes later, as they sat across from one another at the back of the hospital cafeteria, Caleb leaned forward and placed his elbows on the round table. "I see this place more than I like."

With a casual interest, Miranda eyed the shiny new PDA he placed on the table halfway between them and pried off the lid of her cup of coffee, added three containers of cream and a few scoops of sugar. She took a minute to stir and then took a sip. The rich French vanilla flavor felt warm and smooth going down her throat. She knew that it would take at least ten to fifteen minutes for the caffeine to be absorbed into her bloodstream, but just the taste made her feel more alert.

"Thank you, God," she said with a smile on her lips.

His mouth curved upward into a warm grin. "Still not a morning person, are you?"

"Actually, I love mornings. I adore them. I usually get into the office at seven. But this past week has completely disrupted my schedule."

Over the large cup of coffee, Miranda stared at her ex-boyfriend. Years had passed since they'd seen each other, and here they were, after all this time, sitting across from one another like old friends. But they'd never been real best friends. He'd been her soul mate, her first lover, her first love and the last man to break her heart and her trust.

He still looked wonderful—tall, boyish yet distinguished and devastatingly handsome. His skin was a deep earth and his face was clean-shaven with masculine contours and angles. His midnight brows were coal black and finely arched over discerning eyes. She'd seen all the men in his family, and when Caleb reached the age of forty his hair would turn salt-and-pepper, enhancing his already nice-looking face. She'd loved him once, loved him enough to stand up to her brother, enough to overlook his semimanipulative ways and socioeconomic status.

Misgivings and self-doubts she'd thought long buried rose as Miranda remembered meeting Caleb's family and friends for the first time. Although they'd grown up mere miles from one another, it might have been another country for the differences. She'd gone to public school and fought for a scholarship to college; Caleb had graduated from one of the top private high schools in the southeast. She'd lived on campus in a dorm and participated in the work-study program; Caleb lived off campus in a luxury condo.

At the time she'd somehow convinced herself that none of the material things had mattered. What mattered was how she'd felt; and she'd felt more than she could ever imagine. Even when they fought she'd loved him; after breaking up she'd loved him. Only her family had witnessed the fallout from the night she'd shown up at his apartment and seen him with another woman.

She couldn't eat or drink for days. The next

week, after a chance run-in with Caleb's younger brother had left her in tears in the frozen-food aisle of the local grocery store, it became crystal clear she needed to get away. Rescue from her own misery had come in the form of a job offer in D.C. The process of packing up her things, finding a new place to live and moving there allowed for little time to feel sorry for herself. Her work at the Justice Department helped her cope with the loss of the one true love of her life, and her new friendships had helped her smile again.

Still, she'd seen a psychiatrist for a month because Miranda had gotten to the point where she didn't think she could stop loving the man. Shaken with the very memory, she forced her mind to stop and concentrate on the reason she was in the hospital to begin with. "Thank you for saving my brother's life," she rushed.

"Miranda, I haven't earned your gratitude. I wasn't on duty the night your brother was brought into the emergency room."

"Oh."

"But I will be taking over his case and administering treatment for his time in the hospital and if he chooses I can assist with his outpatient rehabilitation and follow-up treatment."

"You put that nicely," she replied with a weak smile. "I think in this matter I won't be giving Darren a choice. I've done my homework and you're the best, Caleb. If you're willing to help, we can't afford to turn you down."

"Did you're research, huh?"

"Some of the nurses couldn't stop singing your praises. They may have been a little biased, but they were honest. You're a good doctor."

"Good luck in convincing Darren of that."

"Don't worry, I can handle my older brother."

"You look great, Miranda."

She took a sip of her coffee. "That's the second time you've said that, Caleb."

His brows rose and then he recalled giving her a compliment during the elevator ride down. "Then it's doubly true."

She placed her cup on the table and sighed. "Look, Caleb. This is really awkward."

"It doesn't have to be. What's past is past, right?"

"Yes and no. It took me a long time to get over what went down between us. And I may have gotten over it, but I can't forget what you did."

Part of him wanted to just give up and let go, but part of him that was practically turning back-flips in enjoyment of Miranda's presence held out hope of getting her back into his life.

"I didn't know she was in my bed that night, Miranda. I thought—"

She cut him off. "That it was me. I know. You told me that a million times. And the truth be told,

I believe you, Caleb. I used that night as an out. We were different and eventually we would have broken up."

"You don't know that."

"Long-distance relationships don't last. You were about to go to Stanford and I didn't want to leave the East Coast. We would have seen each other maybe once a month or less."

"We could have made it work. You could have flown up on a weekend and I could have come down."

She shook her head. They could have made it work on his terms. She would have been more of a trophy girlfriend. They'd had their fiercest fights about money when they were dating. Caleb had plenty of it. He bought her diamond earrings for Christmas, expensive handbags for fun, delivered flowers to her dorm room just because. She may have wanted to go to a local diner for breakfast, but he would pick her up in his BMW and drive up to Buckhead for champagne mimosas and gourmet brunch.

The thing was that it was natural for him and over the top for her. And no matter how many times she tried to communicate it to him, nothing worked. It was insane that she would resent him for spoiling her, for loving her too much, but she had. After spending most of her life under the slightly smothering supervision of her brother and father, she'd wanted to spread her wings more in college. But the deeper they got into the relationship the more Caleb had resembled the men in her family.

She looked at him levelly for a moment and then down at the cup she held in her hand. "That's water under the bridge, Caleb. There's no sense in us resurrecting the past. Why don't we just concentrate on the present?"

"The present." He seemed to stare at her left hand and frowned. The hospital intercom beeped. They heard a doctor being paged to the O.R. Otherwise the quiet murmurs of the other cafeteria patrons drifted into the heavy silence at their table.

"I suppose you want me to forget about what we had?" he said leaning forward.

It wasn't just what Caleb had said, it was the way he said it that had goose bumps pricking the back of Miranda's neck.

"I think that would be best," she said cautiously.

"What kind of lowlife, irresponsible man do you think I am, Miranda? How can you sit there, look me in the eyes and expect me to walk away from her?"

She looked at him and frowned in exasperation. "*Her?* What are you talking about?"

"My daughter," he said, piercing her with his razor-sharp ebony eyes.

Chapter 3

If he had suddenly grown another head and sprouted wings, he couldn't have shocked her more. For long moments, she couldn't speak, couldn't move and could barely even breathe. She felt her mouth hanging slack in an expression attributed to the crazed. "What?"

"You heard me."

"But I don't believe what I heard." Miranda meant to stand up and move away, but before she could move his fingers wrapped around her wrist like a vise. Then, to make it appear as though they were having an intimate conversation, he leaned in close and smiled—a chilling upward turn of his lips she couldn't help but appreciate even though she was still stunned by his accusation.

"You seem surprised," he said, his voice crackling with emotion. "Did you think that I wouldn't find out that you came here with a little girl? A ten-year-old?"

Not only furious but still caught off guard, she ceased struggling, sat back down and took a deep breath. "Let me go, Caleb."

"Tell me about Kelly."

"Fine!" she ground out through clenched teeth. "She looks younger than she really is. Kelly's eleven years old. Ryan and I have cared for her since she was a toddler."

"Ryan?" The menace in Caleb's voice sent a second wave of ice down her spine.

"My ex-husband," Miranda elaborated.

Caleb's gaze darkened and his brows pulled together in a furious frown. "You got married after you left Atlanta?"

Inwardly Miranda shivered. She'd spent over an hour in front of the mirror practicing for this moment, but the reality of his fingers biting into her arm hadn't been part of the rehearsal. She swallowed and barely managed to keep her voice even as she responded. "We met right after I started working in Washington."

"I guess it didn't take you long to find someone

after you left me, did it?" he sarcastically asked. "Makes me wonder if you ever really loved me."

His words were like a kick to her teeth. He thought that she'd never loved him! She'd spent over a year in therapy relearning how to live her life without him. Indignation filled her throat. If she hadn't taken the necessary steps to end their relationship, she would have had to move to California or he would have had to stay out of school for a year and reapply to a medical school in the D.C. area. With either option, they both would have been miserable. The way that Miranda saw it, he should have been thanking her.

"I walked in on you with another woman, Caleb. And after the pain and humiliation dissipated, I forgave you. How dare you question my feelings when I loved you enough to let you go?" she said angrily. "If we'd stayed together, I would have ended up a trophy wife and blamed you for my never having a career."

Caleb released her and placed his fists on the table. His features turned to ice and the dark brown eyes gazing at her were filled with pain and anger. "So I should be grateful to this ex-husband of yours for saving me from a life with you?"

"You should be grateful that I don't slap you," she said. Each word was perfectly and slowly pronounced.

"Miranda—"

She held up a hand. "No, Caleb. I think we've said more than enough. Our relationship ended over eleven years ago. What I did and I am doing after that period is none of your business."

"If the child is mine, then it is my business. I've done nothing but obsess about the way we left things between us. I know that you were angry and you wanted to hurt me. I forgive you. You don't have to lie to me, Miranda. Just tell me the truth. Is she my daughter?"

"I am telling you the truth." The words flew out of her mouth even though her mind called it a lie. For the hundredth time since she'd agreed to take responsibility for Kelly, Miranda was grateful for the drama classes her mother had recommended she take as an elective in high school.

"Miranda," he said with such authority that she froze. "Swear to me that she's not my child."

Not wanting him to think that she was guilty, she met his stare again, righteous indignation exuding from her every pore. "She is my child, not yours. I knew her mother and when she died in a car crash, I was given custody of her daughter because she had no parents and the father was also deceased. The formal adoption only went through last year. I may have thought that you were the scum of the earth for cheating on me, but I've never doubted that you would be a wonderful father for any child and I would never keep a child from their true parents." The last sentence resounded with the truth.

He released her wrists and she snatched them back and began massaging them.

Miranda eyed him warily across the table. His shoulders slumped forward and he looked everywhere but her face. The furrows of his brow deepened and for a split second, she wanted to reach over and soothe them away as she'd done years ago.

"I didn't want to believe that you could do something like that, but…" His voice trailed off.

"But?" she prompted.

"You were so adamant that I forget the past that I thought you wanted to hide her from me."

"Caleb," she gently chided. "I work for the logistics and planning department of the Witness Protection Agency, so I help hide people for a living. Even if I didn't, do you honestly think I would have been dumb enough to show up in this town with a Blackfox child and not have anyone realize her? All it would take is a trip to the grocery store and I would have every member in your family banging on the front door."

He at least had the decency to look embarrassed. "Look, Miranda, I didn't think. I was angry."

"Well get over it, Caleb. I have a sick brother and a little girl to think about. I don't have enough bandwidth to add you to my list right now."

"You're right."

She didn't know if it was her tone or her words that had reached him, but something did. Cautiously, she let go of the breath she'd been holding and pushed her chair back. The wooden legs squeaked on the linoleum floor. "You'll continue as my brother's doctor?" she asked after standing.

"You still want that?"

She nodded. "Sure. I'm going to check in on Darren before I leave. Goodbye, Caleb."

"One last question, Miranda. Did you love him?"

Her breath caught in her throat as she exhaled. He meant Ryan, her fictional ex-husband. She was a good liar, but she wasn't that good. Instead she softly replied, "I trusted him."

And then without another word she left the room.

"My ex-husband."

Caleb inhaled deeply as Miranda turned on her heel and strode out of the cafeteria. All the while his eyes never left the curvaceous backside.

Damn it, she'd walked out on him again. He closed his eyes as anger and disbelief stabbed his gut.

His first love had become some other man's wife. And it was all his fault.

Burying his face in his hands, his mind went

back to that day. Their graduation ceremony was less than two weeks away and he'd just gotten the letter in the mail. After months on the waiting list, he'd been lucky enough to have been accepted into his first-choice medical school. Feeling ready to celebrate, he'd thrown a small party at his place and invited all of his buddies. He'd left messages on Miranda's voice mail and expected her to attend. It hadn't taken much to spread the word. And a few phone calls, along with his American Express card, had secured a number of tables at the local club, top-shelf alcohol and food for the night. After his friends had arrived and the party had started, everything became a messy blur of memories lost in a mix of alcohol.

The next morning, the alarm clock had startled Caleb out of his blissful alcoholic slumber and thrust him into a nightmarish world of pain and regret. When he'd slowly opened his eyes, with relief he'd found himself in his own bed. But the relief quickly disappeared. On the hangover scale of one to ten, his was a fifty. His head felt like a dangerously overinflated basketball being dribbled by a sadistic toddler, and his stomach felt like an octopus getting electrocuted. He sniffed and the smell of smoke and liquor seeped from every pore.

An hour later, after a long shower, he'd finally dragged himself to the kitchen in hopes of getting an aspirin. Just as he crossed the living area, something caught his eye. A bag from his favorite Chinese restaurant, a bottle of wine and a wrapped gift sat on the dining room table. And the fog of the remaining alcohol in his bloodstream cleared as he remembered how he'd gotten home the night before. With precision clarity, he saw his friends dumping him into the backseat of his car and giving Jessica Greene the keys. His gut twisted at the realization that Miranda had possibly walked in before Jessica had left him passed out on the bed.

Caleb got out of his chair and picked up the empty coffee cups. He'd rushed to Miranda's dorm room only to find it empty, and then driven like a maniac to her parents' house. After two weeks of calling and pleading with her family, she'd agreed to see him only to say she never wanted to see him again.

His jaw clenched. Last time he'd walked away. Never again.

Later on that night, after picking Kelly up from her aunt's and returning to the hotel suite, Miranda tucked the child into bed and kissed her on the forehead. As she stared down into her face, a measure of peace returned to her heart. Straightening up, she not only felt a dull pain in her back but also became more aware of her restless state.

Turning around, she walked into the hotel bath-room, closed the door and turned on the water for the bath. Within the few minutes it took to fill the bathtub, she removed her wrinkled clothes and finished her nightly ablution.

Miranda finally climbed into the tub, immersing her body in the hot water. For a moment she stared straight ahead at the steam rising from the water. She closed her eyes and even as her muscles began to relax, her mind continued to hum with the day's events.

Why couldn't he have moved to another state? Why did he have to work in this hospital? Why did he have to be her brother's attending physician?

She blew out an impatient breath. Was this a case of karma, or was it just unfinished business? Whatever the case, she'd recognized the look of determination in Caleb's eyes. Regardless of her wishes, he wasn't going away. Memories of old times drowned out reality. Time spent talking on the phone to the wee hours of the morning, meeting for a quick lunch at their favorite café. She remembered the sight of his smiling face outside her door. She also remembered walks through Piedmont Park holding his hand and acting like kids, spending all day at the amusement park. She caught mental images of being wrapped in Caleb's arms as they had watched old movies and ate popcorn on the couch.

Truthfully, Miranda didn't want him to leave her alone.

She sank even lower into the tub so that her chin almost touched the water. Crossing her arms, she held still, feeling the small ripples. Earlier when she'd told Caleb that she'd believed him years ago when he'd admitted to not sleeping with her worst enemy, she hadn't lied. If someone had ever asked her who she trusted with her life, Caleb would still be on the list.

But no matter how much she'd loved and trusted him then, nothing could change the fact that they were destined to live separate lives. His acceptance to Stanford Medical School and her job offer in Washington, D.C., had forced her to make one of the most difficult and selfish decisions of her life. Even before the night she'd walked in on Caleb and Jessica, she'd had her doubts about their relationship.

Darren's intense dislike of Caleb and her parents' misgivings about the relationship had only increased her doubts. In the end, she'd used Caleb's supposed infidelity as an excuse to push him away.

Miranda sighed and sat up in the bathtub. For a second she heard the heavy footsteps of someone walking down the hotel corridor. Tomorrow, she and Kelly would move into her childhood home. Hopefully within the next two weeks,

Kelly would enroll in the local school and Miranda's brother would be home from the hospital. For the next few months, she wouldn't have to wake up at 5:00 a.m. and take the metro into work, sit in her office working on the computer, attend meetings, or interview. As wonderful as it sounded, she couldn't help but feel a little lost.

Even with everything she faced, she felt good about being back home in a place that filled her with wonderful memories. And there were so many things that hadn't changed. Caleb was just as devastatingly handsome, her brother was still pigheaded and overprotective, and the entire town shut down at ten o'clock. And both she and Caleb were very single, responsible adults.

Correction, she added mentally. According to her altered records, she had an ex-husband and an adopted child. Miranda lifted her hand and stared at the wrinkles in her fingertips. It was way past time for her to get out of the bathtub. After opening the drain, she climbed out of the large tub and wrapped a bath towel around her body. Her muscles had relaxed to the point that she felt like a limp dishrag. Drawing on the last of her energy reserves, she finished drying off and opened her personal cocoa-scented lotion. Mechanically, she smoothed the lotion over her skin. The past is the past, she thought to herself firmly.

You, Miranda Tyler, are a grown, independent

and confident woman. She repeated that statement over and over as she dressed for bed. By the time she reopened the bathroom door and entered the bedroom, she had regained a measure of her former peace. She slid into the bed and curled her arms around the pillow. As sleep came gently she prayed for the strength and fortitude to deal with Caleb Blackfox in the days to come.

Chapter 4

"I don't want you as my doctor, Blackfox."

Caleb looked up from the chart in his hand at the man sitting up in the hospital bed. Ignoring the statement, Caleb slid the hospital door closed.

"You don't have a choice this time, Darren," he replied as if he were announcing the weather. Caleb walked over to the side of the bed and filed back the patient file. Very calmly he reached over and touched Darren's bruised rib.

Completely thrown off by the action, Darren jumped sideways. "Ouch! What the hell are you doing?"

"Checking to see how your ribs are doing. Still cracked I see. Should I check on your arm and leg?"

"Hell, no!"

"My guess is that they are still broken and you need a doctor."

"Yes, I need a doctor. I just don't want you to be that doctor, Blackfox."

Caleb's eyes narrowed and he pulled a pen out of his pocket. His fingers tightened over the metal. "I didn't want Miranda to break up with me and never speak to me again."

"That has nothing to do with me. If my sister wised up and saw you for the playboy you were then that's all your fault."

Caleb looked at the EKG machine and was internally delighted to see Darren's elevated heart rate. In a minute, he expected it to rise even further with his next statement.

"But you see, it isn't my fault because she only saw what you wanted her to see."

"I wasn't involved in your mess, Blackfox."

Anger that he hadn't felt in years rushed from his gut and almost a decade of waiting. "Wrong. You pulled the strings and unless you bury the past here and now I will tell Miranda everything that happened that night and it will bury you."

"You don't know anything. And even if you did—if you told my sister—she didn't believe you ten years ago, what makes you think that she's going to believe you now?"

"Ten years. That's what makes me believe. We were young, stubborn, and both of us wore our hearts on our sleeves then. Now we're older and she will look past the emotions to the facts, Darren."

"Fine, Blackfox, you can be my doctor. But why?"

"Call me Caleb. The Blackfox thing is old, Darren, and I would rather we at least appear on friendly terms. Why am I here? I don't care too much about you and we both know that. I can admire a man who takes care of his own, but you crossed the line. I want to be your doctor because Miranda and I have unfinished business."

"You're going to use my recovery to move back in on my sister? That's low."

Caleb flipped the chart closed after making a few notes. If Darren's recovery progressed as scheduled he would be able to leave the hospital in three days. "No. It's smart. And this conversation is going to guarantee that you don't interfere this time around. If I even catch a hint that you've been whispering in her ear, I will respond swiftly and it won't be nice."

"If you hurt her—" Darren began.

"You're not in a position to make threats," Caleb cut him off. "And now that we've established our new rules, I can get back to being your doctor."

A part of him wanted to ask about the girl, the faceless child that had been in his dreams for the past two days. He wanted to grab Darren by the hospital gown and demand to know if that was his daughter, but he didn't. This was something that he would find out from Miranda and only Miranda. It would hurt him if the child was someone else's, but it would tear him and his family apart if the child were his. The only thing he'd learned as a doctor was to be patient. Now all he had to do was wait for the right time.

"Is everything all right in here?"

Caleb looked up and his eyes met Miranda's. He could tell from the shadows under her eyes that she hadn't slept any better than he had. The sight should have made him feel better, but it didn't. He wondered if it was guilt keeping her up at night.

"Good morning, little sis. Pretty early for you to be visiting, isn't it?"

"Kelly's downstairs getting her physical and didn't need her Mommy hanging around. I thought I'd come up for a second to check up on you."

"Good morning, Miranda."

Her expression cooled slightly when her attention shifted to Caleb. "Hello, Caleb. Is my brother giving you any grief?"

"He's just fine. As a matter of fact, he's on-track for release in a few days."

"Wonderful." She walked over to her brother's bedside and then looked from Darren to Caleb.

Damn, those beautiful eyes of hers could see right through him. Once upon a time it went both ways, but now he couldn't tell what she had going on in that pretty head of hers.

"You must know that we are both grateful for your help."

"Well, the work just started and I've been telling your brother that he's not only going to need someone at home to help take care of him. He'll also need to be under a doctor's supervision. I've volunteered to serve in that capacity."

Miranda's eyes flew to her brother. "And you better have accepted, big brother."

"Hell, I've broken bones, not my head. Yes, I accepted Caleb's offer."

Caleb met Darren's baleful stare. The man continued. "I'd be a fool to turn it down."

"Miracles are happening every day, it seems. Anyway, I'm going back downstairs. I'll be back in about thirty minutes. You want anything, bro?"

"Three chocolate chip cookies, some salted peanuts, a hamburger and a large soda."

"You can have everything but the hamburger and the peanuts. The cafeteria is still serving breakfast," Caleb commented.

"I'll see what I can do." Miranda smiled, turned around and left the room.

Caleb's eyes tracked her through the window, enjoying the nice view of her perfectly endowed backside.

"Man, I can't wait to get out of here," Darren grumbled.

Caleb grinned at the prospect of spending time with Miranda outside of the hospital. "Me, too," he whispered. After making notes on Darren's chart, he left the room and headed for his office. He hadn't forgotten Miranda's primary purpose for being in the hospital. His mind raced with the information.

Trust, but validate.

It was time Caleb found out if he was a father.

Chapter 5

Having spent most of the day moving from the hotel into her parents' house, getting Kelly enrolled in the local junior high school, checking on her brother and settling into the house, Miranda was exhausted.

There were so many memories in the house—all good times she'd savor forever and all of the bad times she couldn't make herself forget. In a way, the bad memories were just as important as the good. Miranda walked down the hallway, her eyes darting over the family photos and bronzed trophies both she and Darren had received in high school. It was amazing that after almost two decades, her mother's favorite crystal vases still shone beautifully underneath the recessed lights.

After turning off all the lights downstairs, she paused in the entry foyer and stared at the fresh orchids in the vase. They had been delivered right after they'd returned from the hospital. The note written in Caleb's almost illegible sprawl was stamped in her mind.

Welcome Home.

It was amazing how two simple words could wreck her concentration. She was here to take care of her brother and hide Kelly, that was it. She didn't come home to renew a failed romance or obsess about what could have been. Shaking her head, Miranda checked the locks, activated the alarm and went upstairs. The sooner she showered, the sooner her head hit the pillow.

She stood on the beach in her dream, dressed in the sheerest cotton. The wind tossed her hair, running through it like a child's fingers. Miranda looked out at the sun as it began its gradual descent, casting a spell over the water. The deep blue glittered like gold. She felt the warmth of his arm around her shoulders.

As they walked along the shore, palm trees swaying with the night breeze seemed to urge them forward along the path. The sand had begun to shimmer and the gentle waves tickled her feet as the foam ran over their toes. Sounds of the surf mixing with the cooing of birds formed a beautiful lullaby. And she was with him. Could anything be better than this? Miranda rested her cheek on his chest and was wrapped in his arms.

His scent seemed to encircle her. His essence lay over her skin like a fine mist. As they stood together, past and future seemed to be laid out before them in brilliant colors of happiness and peace. Life without his smile seemed empty and shallow.

When he spoke, she smiled. His voice, so deep and gentle, was filled with affection.

"Miranda, you are more beautiful than all women and more precious than any rose. I wake in the morning with thoughts of you on my mind. 'What can I do to make her smile? What words may I say to make her stay with me? How can I heal her hurts? Gain her trust?' I want to protect you, love you. For you I would give everything I possess, for your love would make me the happiest man in the entire world. I beg of you, dear sweet Miranda, will you…"

She stood watching as he began to bend down on one knee.

"Yes?"

"Miranda, would you…"

"Miranda!"

"Yes," she muttered before opening her eyes.

Kelly stood next to the bed. She cradled a note-book in her hands and looked over at Miranda like she was a lunatic.

"Sorry."

"No, it's okay." She rubbed the sleep out of her eyes before looking at the alarm clock—5:45 a.m. "Kelly, why are you up and dressed so early?"

"I don't want to be late to my first day of school."

"You have to be there by eight-fifteen."

"I know, but the bus will be here at seven fifty-five and you said yesterday that you wanted to make breakfast. If we start now, you can shower, make breakfast, we can do the dishes and have time left over to watch the news."

Miranda blinked as her mind struggled to get into gear. And when she finished processing all the information, her amazement grew a hundredfold. The power of genetics stared at her from Kelly's light brown eyes. The child was her father's clone. She couldn't imagine a more organized, systematic, careful and efficient Federal Marshal than Ryan.

"I should have known you were a morning person," Miranda said shaking her head. She was doomed to spend her life surrounded by them.

"Come on," Kelly took her hand. "It won't be that bad. You don't even have to make me waffles. I'm more of a pancakes kind of girl anyway. I can show you how my mom used to make smiley faces with blueberries," she cajoled.

Miranda couldn't help but giggle at the bright smile on Kelly's face. "You were lucky. My mom's the worst cook. I remember when she burnt the toast and started a grease fire one Sunday when frying bacon."

"Daddy tried to cook an egg in the microwave and it exploded," Kelly chimed in as they walked to the hallway.

"Darren killed the coffeepot."

They looked at each other and burst out laughing. Miranda laughed so hard tears spurted from her eyes and her side hurt.

"See. I knew I could do it," Kelly bragged.

"Do what?"

"Get you out of the bed."

Miranda snorted. "Good job. Your father would be proud."

"Yeah, I can't wait to tell him."

Reaching over to tweak one of Kelly's two braids, she smiled. "He'll call tonight. Now let me get ready. I don't want Ryan's little marshal late for her first day of school."

"She's fine, Ryan. Kelly is a resilient little girl. She worries about you, but other than that I think she's going to be fine in school," she reassured the Federal Marshal on the phone.

Thankful for the Bluetooth wireless headset that allowed her free use of her arms, Miranda continued wiping off the kitchen countertops. Although she'd hired a maid service to spruce up the house, she still felt the need to do her own bit of cleaning.

"I hope to God this trial ends soon."

Miranda had known Ryan for over four years, and in that time together she had never seen the agent without a can-do attitude and an impenetrable veneer of confidence. Ryan Walker always got his man or woman. And now he was a client of the very system of which he was a member. Two months ago, his entire life was once again turned upside down as the Russian Mafia somehow discovered the location of a safe house where Ryan was hiding an informant. With his principal gunned down execution-style, Ryan was the only living witness to the murder. His testimony alone would ensure the conviction of Sergey Milonik, the head of Russian-American mafia's largest crime syndicate.

Inwardly, Miranda sighed. It didn't seem fair that at the point where Ryan and Kelly had just seemed to be completely healed from his wife's death from leukemia, he would have to go into witness protection and be separated from his daughter.

"Have you given any more thought as to where

you're going to relocate once Milonik is in prison?" she asked.

"That's all I've thought about since this mess started. It's been an eye-opening experience being on the other side of the table, Miranda. My life will never be the same."

"It can be a good thing, Ryan. You've been mentioning lately that you want to spend more time with Kelly."

"Sounds like that old adage—Be careful what you wish for…"

"You might just get it," she finished.

Ryan's laughter traveled well over the phone line and Miranda smiled at the thought that she'd been able to provide some glimmer of humor for her friend.

"Yeah. Well, if things go as planned I'll be down there for my girl within the next two months."

"Are they going to make you fly blind or are you getting to have a say in where they're going to resettle the two of you?"

"We're working on that. Everybody knows that my case won't follow strict protocol and I'm pushing hard for it to be. I'll take the change in identity, the new career and the relocation. But I refuse to sacrifice my daughter's happiness."

Miranda stared out the kitchen window to look over the backyard. Instead of the patches of fallen leaves and naked trees, she pictured her mother's garden in the middle of summer. With that happy thought in her mind, she optimistically declared, "It will all work out, you'll see."

"Your lips to God's ears. Tell Kelly I love her and I'll talk to her soon."

"Promise."

"Take care."

The line went silent. Miranda pulled the slender phone from her pocket and made sure to erase all of her incoming calls just as an extra precaution. Deciding to go ahead and finish up her preparation for dinner that night, she had just opened the refrigerator when the doorbell to her parents' house rang.

Miranda's brow wrinkled. She hadn't expected anyone in the middle of the day. Still cautious from all the stories she'd heard from the field, she peered through the blinds and her confusion doubled at the sight of the luxury SUV in her driveway. Could it be one of her brother's friends? Wouldn't they know that he wasn't scheduled to be discharged from the hospital until tomorrow?

Miranda glanced into the peephole and her heart skipped a couple of beats before moving into overdrive. After running her fingers through her hair and pinching her cheeks, she opened the door. "Caleb. I wasn't expecting you."

He grinned and held up a shopping bag. "I was just in the neighborhood and decided to stop by. Aren't you going to invite me in?"

Miranda eyed him suspiciously. "Of course."

Caleb closed the door and slowly strolled to the center of the entry hallway. "The place looks great."

"Thank you."

"The last time I was here your parents were teasing you about having to work until their sixties to pay for college tuition. I can't believe they're retired and teaching in Africa."

"Believe it or not, neither can I. Imagine my mother without all the accoutrements of civilization?" Miranda shook her head and chuckled. "It's a little unbelievable."

"Are they doing okay?"

"They're great. According to my father, it's been like a second wind for their marriage."

Miranda shook her head and remembered her manners. "Can I offer you something to drink?"

"Anything with caffeine would be greatly appreciated."

"Long night?"

"It never ended. We had a staff shortage so I pulled another double."

"Why aren't you at home?"

"Because I needed to talk with you. I don't like the way we left things yesterday and I wanted to apologize in person."

Miranda could barely swallow past the lump in her throat. Of all the things she'd expected this morning, this had surely been the last; that simply hearing Caleb say he was sorry would show her how deeply, how easily he still affected her.

She came to a stop in the kitchen and turned. "You don't have to apologize."

"Well, let's just say that I don't apologize, but I would like to start over and I've a peace offering." He held up the shopping bag. "I hope you haven't had lunch. I brought food. We could practice the old-school way of making up by breaking bread together."

"There's old school and old testament." Miranda smiled, crossing her arms over her chest.

Caleb grinned and began to take items out of the bag. "Hungry?"

"Well, I did skip breakfast this morning."

"Most important meal of the day," Caleb quipped.

"Which I am sure you skipped as well." Miranda aimed a sidelong glance toward the man at her side. She reached into the cabinet and pulled out plates and glasses.

"Guilty as charged."

His grin bloomed wide. In that instance Miranda took in his deep dimple, killer smile and gorgeous brown eyes. Damn, Caleb was good-looking. Her mother had always warned her that looks could be deceptive and she'd discovered the veracity of that advice many a time. But none of that seemed to matter as her pulse rocketed upward. She lowered her eyes and bit the inside of her lip.

There were some men who took their looks seriously and she would have never known until a few of her girlfriends complained that their boyfriends spent more time in the bathroom and shopping malls than they did. Caleb could have been one of those men.

Even in college he always looked good. His shirts freshly pressed, suits perfectly tailored. As he stood in her parents' kitchen in a wool turtleneck and jeans, with the shadow of stubble on his strong jaw, heat began to spiral to all parts of her body. Her eyes locked with his grinning brown ones and Miranda blushed at being caught staring. With a death grip on the plates, she swung around and headed for the table. She was in trouble.

Big trouble.

Much later after they'd eaten lunch and cleaned up the dishes, Miranda leaned against the countertop across from Caleb.

"I know that I'm not your favorite person right now, but I need to ask a favor," Caleb announced.

Even after over two hours of friendly conversation and laughter, Miranda tensed at his statement. "Go ahead."

"Kiss me, Miranda. Just once. I need to know if I'm alone in feeling this chemistry or if you feel it, too."

"I don't think that would be a good idea."

"Thinking. That's what we've always done. We're adults now and I need to know if it's just the memories or if this is real."

"Why don't we just assume it's the memories and leave it alone?"

Caleb's brow rose and he crossed his arms over his chest. "Scared?"

"Of what?"

"Admitting that you want me just as much as I want you."

"Get over yourself."

Caleb chuckled. "I'm sorry, but I know you, Miranda. You may have grown beautiful, but I can tell when you're afraid."

"I'm not afraid of you."

"Prove it."

"Fine."

Her heart skipped a couple of beats as she forced herself to look him in his eyes. She blushed and her tongue darted out over her suddenly dry lips. She couldn't have said no even if she'd wanted to. She rose on tiptoes and lightly brushed his bottom lip with her own. His lips were firm and tender.

Of their own accord her hands found purchase on his shoulders and her eyes closed and his arms wrapped around her, and her mouth opened underneath his, deepening their kiss. Liquid fire raced up and down her spine while her pulse quickened until it was thunder in her veins. Only Caleb had ever made her feel such passion, to make her forget everything but the touch of his hands on the small of her back, holding her body closer to his as she felt the heat of his kiss.

He slanted his mouth across hers, his tongue slid deep into her mouth. Miranda moaned deep and low in her throat as the hot, wet sensation sent a jolt through her body.

Caleb drew away, but Miranda still held on to his shoulders because he'd stolen her breath and knocked her off balance. Lord, it felt good. She reveled in his kiss, his mouth, his scent. He smelled and tasted like steamy fantasies and healthy man. Hot and firm, yet tender, his lips moved over hers with gentle gliding motions.

He settled his lips on the corner of her mouth and teased her bottom lip with his teeth. "God, you're sweet, Miranda. It's been a lifetime since I've tasted you."

She opened her eyes. He was staring down at her, eyes hooded and dark with arousal. Miranda returned his stare and blinked a few times as she found herself in the one place she'd sworn she'd never be again—Caleb's arms. A trickle of fear cleared away the remaining haze from her sluggish mind.

"It's still there, baby," he murmured against her mouth. "Sweet Jesus, I have missed you so much."

"It doesn't change anything," she said in a shaky voice. "It can't change anything."

Before she could move away, Caleb lifted her captive hand to his mouth and slowly ran his lips over her skin, his eyes never leaving hers. She shivered.

"Baby, this changes everything," he said. His voice was low and commanding, sending more tremors through her. Dumbstruck, all she could do was watch as he left the house.

Chapter 6

Normally at eight o'clock on a Friday night, Caleb would have been sitting at a dinner table in an exclusive Atlanta restaurant dining with a beautiful companion. Today, however, as he sat back in his leather chair and stared out his office window, all he wanted was to be in bed.

Correction, Miranda's bed.

With a sigh, he closed his eyes and pictured her slender arms, long legs and silky smooth skin. It was amazing that only a week had passed since she'd stepped into his life. In the beginning, when he'd made the decision to remain impervious to the attraction, he'd had every intention of remaining in control. It was seeing her day in and day out at the hospital, getting close but not too close. Touching her on the back, her cheek, smelling her perfume, the hungry glances and the subsequent denials. He'd thought that he was attracted to her when they'd been in a relationship years ago, but this was another story. He couldn't get her out of his head.

Only in his deepest concentration, while examining his patients, did he find a measure of peace. Yet once he stepped out of a hospital room or away from a hospital bed, Miranda was there. With his eyes closed, Caleb raised his hand and rubbed his neck. If he were a psychologist, he would come damn close to diagnosing his current state of mind as obsessive.

He lowered his gaze and stared blankly at a stack of patient files. He was falling hard. Again. As much as he didn't want to admit it, it hadn't taken much time. A part of him had never gotten over Miranda. If he was completely honest with himself, she was probably the reason that he hadn't been able to commit to any of the women who'd briefly shared his life and his bed.

Caleb jumped at the chirp of his cell phone. Reaching over, his brow wrinkled when he glanced at the caller identification. It indicated the call was from Marius. Pressing the send key, he brought the phone to his ear. "I thought you were in Brussels this week."

Not only was Marius his older brother, but he was also the CEO of Blackfox Industries. Growing up, Marius had taken to the role of eldest sibling like a duck to water. If anything went wrong, and none of them wanted their parents to know about it, they went to Marius. As much as Caleb had resented the attention Marius had received from both his father and grandfather, he was entirely grateful it wasn't him. Started over a half century ago, Blackfox Industries, a family-owned trucking company, had been run by his grandfather.

And as the history went, for the past two generations, it had been the second son who'd run the company. His older brother was the *first* firstborn Blackfox son to run the company; and if business kept up they were headed toward the best year on record. Being the second child in his family, Caleb had been lucky to escape that fate. The funny thing was that Marius always said that he didn't know how Caleb could function as a doctor, knowing that he held someone's life in his hands. Well he could say the same thing back to his older brother. Hundreds of people depended upon his brother's ability to manage their corporation. Not to mention that Blackfox Industries was also a privately held company that still continued to run as if it were a family-owned business. For Marius, work equated with family, and no matter the personal sacrifice he would place it first.

Marius's normally deep voice came through the airwaves raspy. "I'm not feeling so hot. I almost passed out before getting on the plane and threw up in the bed."

Caleb sat forward. "Did you call a doctor?"

"Did I call a doctor?" Marius repeated. "Yeah, I'm on the phone with the wiseass right now."

"Hey, hey." Caleb laughed. "I'm your brother first and doctor second. What are your symptoms?"

"Chills, sore throat, headache, chest aches, sore muscles, stuffy nose and I have cayenne peppers for eyeballs."

Caleb frowned as his mind ran through the list of his symptoms in an attempt to narrow down the possible diagnosis.

"Are you running a fever?"

"How the hell should I know?"

"Pull out a thermometer."

"Why don't you pick one up at the hospital?"

"I'd be more than happy to grab you a couple of extra. I can get a three-for-one on the rectal kind."

"Bro, did a patient throw up on you or something?"

"It's not work."

"If it's not work, then what is it? Because I know it can't be a woman."

For a moment Caleb remained silent. Marius

was right. He was in a rotten mood because of a female. No, two females. Within the next twenty-four hours, he would find out whether or not he was a father and if the woman that he loved was lying to him.

"I've just got some things on my mind."

"It is a woman." Marius's announcement ended with a spurt of coughing. "What's her name?"

Caleb's stomach growled, reminding him that he was coasting on the fumes of a sausage, biscuit and coffee breakfast. "I'll be over in a half hour. Got food at your place? And I'm not talking about beer, milk and cereal."

"Yeah, Marie dropped off some meals yesterday."

This time his stomach let out a howl that would have put any one of his littler brother's canine patients to shame. Marie was their parents' live-in cook and housekeeper. Caleb had tried every trick in the book, and then some that he'd made up, to get her to cook for him. Just the thought of her pot roast made him weak in the knees. It was a long-standing family mystery as to how Marius had convinced her to cook extra portions and deliver them to his older brother's freezer.

Cradling the phone between his ear and his shoulder, Caleb stood up and began to unbutton his white doctor's coat. "Throw a couple of them in the oven. I'll be over in fifteen minutes."

It took Caleb longer to make his way through the hospital and out the front doors than it took for him to drive to Marius's place. As he confidently maneuvered the Lexus around the tight curves of the country roads, he eased back into the leather seat and smiled. The purr of the car's engine and quick responsiveness justified all the grief his Ford-car-dealership uncle gave him at the family gatherings. If he'd wanted a truck, he would have gone to his uncle. But he'd needed a luxury car that was dependable as well as precise.

He turned the last corner and passed through the ornate stone entranceway into the executive neighborhood. Like clockwork, he couldn't help but roll his eyes. Caleb and Marius had overseen the construction of the mansion, and he could still remember the reactions of the neighborhood: half in awe and the other in depression. His oldest brother had more than broken the color barrier—he'd shattered every stereotype.

After pulling into the driveway, he parked on the pavement outside the three-car garage. A minute later, with his medical bag in hand, Caleb strolled through the two-story foyer and headed toward the back of the house. Just as he expected, Marius was ensconced in his office, staring at the large flat-panel computer screen.

Standing in the entranceway, he watched as

Marius rubbed the bridge of his nose. "Don't you ever take a break?"

"Don't you ever knock?"

"Why knock when you've got a key?"

"I can remedy that situation."

"Whatever." Caleb grinned. As much as he hated to see his brother sick, he enjoyed the hell out of being the one to come to the rescue instead of being rescued.

"Say *ahh*," Caleb ordered as he shined a penlight into Marius's mouth.

"Do I have the flu?"

Caleb shook his head after flicking off the light. The lack of a fever was all he needed to know before diagnosing the condition. "No, looks like you have a severe sinus infection."

"All right. Give me antibiotics and the telephone. I can re-book my flight and at least attend two days of the conference."

"If you get on a plane in your condition, you could blow your eardrums to shreds. You're damn lucky you didn't get on the flight this morning. We've seen some cases at the hospital where sinus membranes have torn from the air pressure."

Marius grimaced before reaching up to rub the bridge of his nose. "How long am I grounded?"

"You'll be out of action as long as your sinus passages look like moldy Swiss cheese."

"Appreciate the visual, bro."

"Anytime."

Caleb reached into his medical bag and pulled out two prescription bottles. "Here's the antibiotic to clear up the infection, and this will help drain your sinus passages. Be careful not to take these close to bedtime or you'll be memorizing the ceiling at three in the morning."

"I thought you were here to cure me, not give me insomnia."

"Cause and effect. The sleeplessness is a side effect of the antihistamine." His stomach growled, reminding him that he hadn't eaten in a while. "Dinner ready, yet?"

Marius stood up and they walked toward the rear of the house. "Yeah, I left your plate in the oven. I already ate."

Caleb must have had a betrayed look on his face as Marius shrugged. "You took too long."

"Thanks for waiting," he responded sarcastically.

They made their way down the hallway and passed through the spacious living room before entering the gourmet kitchen. As the CEO of a large company, Marius's surroundings fit his stature in life. The sprawling modern-style estate housed numerous rooms, a home theater, basketball court, swimming pool and other rewards of success. Caleb knew the layout of the house almost better than he knew his own. They both had used the same architect to design their homes and Caleb had lived there while his own house was being built.

After pulling out cutlery and pouring a glass of iced tea, he turned off the gas oven, reached for an oven mitt and carefully removed the meal. The scent of roasted meat almost made him dizzy. Dropping the small pan on a plate, he brought it over to the table and sat down. He said a quick prayer, and picked up his fork and knife. The first bite with the meaty prime rib and thick gravy made everything in the world look good. So good he was still chewing when he went back for a second bite.

"Don't they feed you at that hospital?"

Although still starving, Caleb retained enough of his manners to finish chewing and swallowing before responding to his brother. "Who has time to eat?"

"Apparently not you, little brother."

"There's a nasty stomach virus going around. A few of the doctors were out today and there was a chain wreck of accidents on the highway this morning."

"So who's the lady?"

Caleb gave Marius a questioning glance, and then took a long drink of iced tea. "What lady?"

"The lady who has made you deaf and put you in such a foul mood."

"You're not going go let it drop, are you?"

"I could ask Mom."

Damn. Caleb's shoulders slumped with defeat. If another sibling had made that threat, he wouldn't have believed them, but Marius rarely bluffed. "Miranda Elizabeth Tyler."

Marius sat down across from him. The walnut breakfast table gleamed under the light. His eyes locked on Caleb's like a laser beam. "I've heard her name before."

Caleb took a swig of tea before answering. "We dated in college."

"Oh, that Miranda." Marius tapped his finger against the table. "The same one you took on the skiing trip, went to school at Spellman, grew up about ten miles from our parents' house and has an older brother who hated your guts? The same one that broke up with you after walking into your apartment and finding the half-naked homecoming queen in your bed? The one who messed you up so bad, that we had to pull you out of the bottom of a dozen Hennessy bottles?"

Caleb's shoulders slumped a little more with each item added to the list. By the time Marius finished summing up their relationship history, he looked like the Hunchback of Notre Dame. "Yeah, that Miranda. She's back in town to help her brother recover from a car accident."

"Walk away, little brother," Marius cautioned before coughing.

"I wish I could." Caleb sighed putting down his fork and knife. "I wish I could," he repeated.

An hour later as they sat ensconced in the den, Caleb leaned back in the sleek black leather recliner and relaxed. The combination of a full stomach, and a half glass of premium scotch had more than taken the edge off his day. "I'm going to get her back, bro."

Marius turned his attention from the flat-screen television.

Caleb raised a hand. "Wait, wait. Don't give me that look."

"What look? The one that says you're about to make a big mistake or the one that says you should know better?"

"I do know better this time and I'm going to make this work. I know she has feelings for me, and the chemistry…" Caleb licked his lips as the memory of kissing her in the kitchen flashed through his mind. "More powerful than it was ten years ago."

"Yeah, yeah. The question is—how do you think that you can get around her brother this time?"

"Darren knows that I know that he set me up."

"And you think he won't do it again? You think that after her brother's recovery is finished that Miranda won't leave you like she did last time?"

"The last time I should have followed. The last

time was partially my fault. This time there's more than my precious ego involved. There's the child."

Marius sat up and his eyes narrowed. "Child?"

"Miranda didn't come back alone. She has a daughter. Kelly." Caleb rubbed his head as fury raced up and down his spine. The clinical, reasonable part of his mind understood and could reason out why she wouldn't tell him that he was a father. The other side couldn't deal with the fact that someone he loved could be so cruel.

"Jesus, Caleb. Are you telling me that I have a niece? That Mom and Dad have a granddaughter?"

"No… Yes… I don't know. Miranda says that the little girl is adopted and I don't want to think she would lie to me. But it can't be a coincidence that Kelly's eleven years old."

"So what are you going to do?"

"I've already sent off a DNA sample to the lab. I should get the results in the morning."

"She agreed to let you take a DNA test?"

"Miranda doesn't know about it. She had to get a full physical for her daughter before enrolling her in school. I pulled some strings and managed to get a blood sample."

Marius's eyebrows shot upward and his lips curved into a grin. "I'm impressed."

"Don't be," Caleb responded. "What I did was not only unethical, it could get me fired."

"If the girl's yours?" Marius rasped.

Caleb's jaw ticked at the thought and his finger tightened on the glass of scotch single malt. His life would change; it already had. He'd further decrease his schedule at the hospital to spend more time with Miranda and Kelly. Next, he'd start construction on a new house near his parents. He'd already picked out an architect and an interior designer.

As his firstborn, Kelly would have the biggest bedroom and he'd give her a computer room next to his study. Miranda would have her own set of rooms for any daytime activities, but he would stipulate that they would sleep in the same bed. If the tests came back and he *was* Kelly's father, the one missing piece of his life would be filled. And if they came back and he wasn't her father…?

Caleb lifted the crystal glass to his lips and swallowed hard. The rich, smoky flavor warmed his throat. No matter the outcome, he wanted Miranda. He wanted to talk to her about his life since she'd left, share with her his good days and his bad days. He wanted to listen to her tell him about her life before and after becoming Kelly's mother. He wanted to know her hopes, her dreams and desires. He wanted to come home from the hospital to her every night, talk about their days and hear her thoughts. "You might want to stay in town next week, because there's going to be a wedding."

Somehow Marius read his mind. "And if Miranda is telling the truth and the girl is adopted?"

He set the glass down lightly on the side table and compared the last week—with Miranda and Kelly in his life—to the years he'd been alone.

He'd been downright arrogant on the last few dates he'd had. The women were beautiful, intelligent and available. Syleena and Diane. They both worked in the medical field, came from good families. Whenever he needed female company for an event, dinner, or physical companionship, he called and vice versa. It had been established early on that none of them were looking for full-time relationships.

But now things had changed; he'd changed. He didn't want to be the bachelor doctor anymore.

Chapter 7

"Ms. Tyler do you have a minute?"

"Of course," Miranda responded as she stopped a few feet from Darren's hospital room. The nurses had assured her that it would take a few hours for them to complete the full battery of tests. In the meantime, she'd planned to run across the street and get something to eat.

She turned to see a lighter-skinned black woman in a black pantsuit approaching her from the nurses' station. Her brow creased. Whoever she was, she didn't appear to be a doctor. Not that Miranda expected all the doctors to be men or older white women. But the lady's skin glowed, her clothing was extremely stylish and her appearance didn't seem in keeping with the eighteen-hour days practiced by many of the hospital doctors. "We haven't met yet, but my name is Grace Samson and I hope to be your brother's physical therapist."

Miranda stuck out her hand and the other woman shook it. "Please call me Miranda."

"Now I just need your help. Caleb predicted your brother wouldn't be too keen on having physical therapy and he's even less agreeable that this therapist is female."

Miranda closed her eyes and shook her head in embarrassment. If ever she had wondered why her brother had yet to settle down with a woman or even have a steady girlfriend, she had her answer. "I'm sorry. My brother can be…" Her voice trailed off.

"He's old school and a little stubborn."

Miranda smiled and nodded her head. "Exactly."

"Is he this prejudiced against doctors or is it that I'm female?"

Miranda shook her head. "He's not fond of doctors, but Darren loves women. It's just that he's such a workaholic that he never meets them."

"One thing's for sure, I could use your help getting around that gruff exterior."

Very smooth, Miranda thought to herself. She

would have used a completely different sentence. Something more along the lines of—"how do I knock some sense into that hardheaded mule?"

"What have you tried?" Miranda questioned.

"I introduced myself and told him that Dr. Blackfox had asked me to oversee his outpatient recovery."

Miranda winced. After the mere mention of Caleb's name, Darren had probably made up his mind to dismiss Grace. "Believe me when I say that my brother's attitude had nothing to do with you."

"I find that hard to believe."

Miranda shook her head. "Darren has never liked Caleb. And the fact that Caleb is his doctor is like a thorn in his side."

"I should have known." Grace laughed before continuing. "Male ego."

"Exactly." Miranda joined in the laughter.

Grace nodded and the two of them glanced toward the empty hospital room at the same time. "So do you have any ideas on how I can get a little cooperation from him?"

Miranda tapped her finger against her cheek and stared as another patient was wheeled down the hallway. After a few minutes of silence, she smiled. "Next time ask how long he's willing to wait to get his life back. And if that doesn't work, threaten him with the idea that he won't be able to play his video games with his right hand."

Grace's thoughtful expression transformed to a full grin. "So it's 'go for his weakness'?"

"Exactly," Miranda replied as they both started walking toward the elevator. She looked down at Grace's left hand and was relieved to find her ring finger bare.

Grace looked at her watch, and then back at the file in her hand. "Any other things I might need to know before I see him in two hours?"

Miranda pressed the elevator button and then turned to look at Grace with a mischievous glint in her eyes. "He's a big Tennessee Titans fan, cooks, folds laundry, takes out the garbage, and although he'll never admit it, Darren loves kids."

Miranda glimpsed the look of shock in Grace's eyes and laughed. It was way past time her brother had someone in his life, and if he wouldn't take the initiative and talk to the beautiful physical therapist, then it fell upon her to do so.

Miranda turned around as she heard the elevator doors slide open and her eyes widened. The man she'd been thinking about all day stood in the elevator.

"Caleb," she said, and glanced back toward Grace, only to find the woman waving a hand and walking away. Miranda's shoulders slumped a little. She was on her own with this one.

"Miranda," he said simply.

Toying with her purse strap, she stepped aside

to allow a nurse access to the elevators. "Darren's not in his room. They took him down for tests."

"I know. We discussed it this morning. If the X-rays and scans come out clean, he gets to go home. If not he'll be here for another night."

Her eyes narrowed on his face. "So how did you do it?"

"Do what?"

"Convince my brother, president of the anti-Blackfox fan club, to cooperate with you on his recovery, and agree to a physical therapist as well. Sarcastic comments and threats aside, he's being halfway civil."

"It must be my bedside manner."

Miranda raised an eyebrow.

"How about my outstanding reputation in the medical community?"

"Enough. You don't want to tell me the real reason. I get that. What I don't get is why you volunteered to treat him. He once gave you a bloody nose and a black eye."

"True, but he was protecting his little sister. I would have done the same for Regan."

She shook her head. "It still doesn't explain it."

"Let me help. I messed up one of the greatest things in my life when I let you go. You're here for a limited time, so I intend to spend as much time as I can getting to know you again, Miranda Tyler."

"I'm not the girl I used to be, Caleb."

"I saw that the first moment I saw you the first day at the hospital. When we were together in college, you were a pretty girl. Now you're a stunning woman."

"Some things haven't changed. You still have a silver tongue."

"I'm a little rusty. But now that you're back I can practice."

She was unwilling to admit that his flattery was getting him somewhere. Actually his eyes were making her temperature go up. Miranda cleared her throat, and then aimed a pointed glance in the direction of her brother's empty hospital suite. "Darren should be back soon."

"He won't be back for a few hours. Besides I wasn't looking for your brother. I was looking for you."

"Oh, what can I do for you?"

That sentence took on a whole new meaning for Caleb as he watched Miranda's tongue glide across her lower lip. There were so many things that he would love to do to her. The first would be taking her to his office, locking the door and making up for years of lost time.

Whatever doubts he'd had about Miranda had disappeared in the morning when he'd opened the DNA report. According to the results, Kelly did not share a genetic relationship with either he or Miranda. It not only confirmed that she was telling the truth, it also reconfirmed his conviction that he wanted to have a family. Knowing that Miranda wouldn't be ready to hear that yet, he settled for something more practical. "You can come to lunch with me. We can talk about your brother and I have a little project I could use your help on. I know of this nice Italian restaurant a few miles from here."

Miranda looked at her watch. "Wow, look at how time has flown. I should run out and take care of some errands before bringing Darren home."

"You have two hours."

"I can drive fast."

"This town moves slowly. You're running again, Miranda."

"Look, Caleb, when you're around me I get confused and although part of me wants to pick up where we left off, I can't…correction, we can't."

"Can I see your left hand?" he asked.

Her eyes narrowed. Fighting a wave of panic, she managed to slow her erratically thumping heart. They were standing in the middle of a semi-busy hospital corridor with more than a few eyes on them, but she still felt as nervous as walking through an alley after midnight. Unbidden, her eyes landed on his lips. The same lips that had given her more sexual fulfillment in sixty seconds than she'd had in years. A shiver ran up and down her spine. "Why?"

"Humor me."

She raised her left hand and he held it within his own. Memories flashed through his mind of her fingertips grazing over his skin, her soft palms resting against his chest. Her fingers intertwined with his as she neared her climax. Pushing the thoughts away he concentrated on remembering the point he was trying to make. "You're not wearing a wedding ring."

"No, I'm divorced, but you knew that."

"Yes, but the lack of a ring on your finger or mine means I have a chance, Miranda. That is, unless you tell me there's someone else."

As soon as the words left his mouth, Caleb gave serious thought to the fact that Miranda did have an ex-husband and, for however long, they shared custody of a child. A child that he wished was his, but the test results proved she was not. No one in his family had yet to divorce or go through the emotional drama of sharing custody, but he'd witnessed the powerful bonds divorced couples shared.

He gripped her hands. "Is there someone else, Miranda?"

She shook her head. "There is no one else."

"But me," he added with a smile.

"I didn't say that."

"But you will. Now let's go get lunch."

Chapter 8

"I want to go on record that this is a bad idea," Miranda grumbled.

"Going to lunch with a beautiful woman when I have a line of consults starting at two o'clock? Very bad idea, but I'm willing to risk it." Caleb pressed the elevator call button and stood at Miranda's side. The scent of her perfume wafted to his nose and he was damn glad to have on his doctor's coat. As they walked down the hallway he noticed that many female and male heads turned to watch and stare as they left the building.

Caleb reached into his pocket and steered Miranda toward the reserved parking deck.

"I thought you said it was across the street," she said.

"Across the main street and down a few blocks. On a nice day, I would walk it, but since it's a little cold outside, it's better if we take a car."

He caught her worried look.

"Don't worry. I'll have you back before your brother gets restless. But I can guarantee that there'll be a pool going with your name as the main contender for the title of Dr. Blackfox's girl."

"You have a very high opinion of yourself, don't you, Caleb."

"Actually, I have the gift of observation," Caleb explained. "I've been trying to get you alone for the past few days, but you're either arriving or leaving when I come around to check up on Darren. Not to mention that there's been an increase in the number of nurses requesting to be assigned to the station covering your brother."

"And all that translates to?"

Caleb eyed Miranda carefully. Though obviously intrigued, she looked ready to run at any moment.

"All of this means that you're avoiding me. I want you, and everyone at the hospital is going to take bets on the undoing of Dr. Blackfox."

He pressed the button to unlock the doors to the Mercedes SUV and opened the passenger side door. Their eyes locked. With the bright winter light warming her face, Miranda's eyes were stunning. And the absence of the French twist made his fingers itch to touch her hair.

"Am I your undoing, Caleb?" she asked.

There was a hum of amusement in her voice and the corner of his mouth hitched up a little higher. "Let me make it plain. When we were together years ago, we were good together. Now? You're still the most gorgeous woman I've ever met. You have a smile that could melt a polar ice cap and you have the sexiest eyes that light up whenever those deliciously perfect lips break into a smile."

He reached out and ran his fingertips lightly across her cheek. "You've got a scent that can drive a man crazy," he said, moving closer to whisper in her ear. Giving in to temptation, Caleb kissed her neck gently and Miranda sighed, leaning into his body. She was soft, sweet and warm. All the things he was missing in this life. He wanted to wrap his hands around her body and kiss her until they both ran out of air. But the cold wind and the sound of a car engine turning over brought him back to reality. "So to answer your question, sweetness," he whispered close to her ear. "I'm already undone."

He pulled back and smiled into her wide-eyed stare. "You…are not serious," she stammered.

"I am more serious about you than anything else in my life. Now let's have lunch."

Caleb held out his hand and assisted her into the Benz. After closing the door he let out a sigh and gave himself a pat on the back. Undone, unhinged, unglued. But with Miranda in his life...

At least he wouldn't be unhappy.

"Welcome to the best Italian restaurant north of Atlanta," Caleb announced as he opened the restaurant's door.

If he'd told her the sky was lavender and world peace could come from the bottom of a Cracker Jack box, Miranda would have believed him. In the space of half a mile, Caleb Blackfox had managed to erase over ten years of distance. Even fate seemed to be working in his favor. It was the only way she could rationalize how their "favorite" song happened to be playing on the radio.

"Thank you," Miranda said as she walked through the small doorway of a restaurant named Bella. Immediately upon stepping into the building, she caught the scent of bread from the oven, olive oil, garlic and herbs.

The host greeted them as Caleb stepped into the foyer. He was a small man with a cute little mustache, little creases around his eyes and laugh lines. He led them past crowded tables to seat them at a nice secluded one in the back corner of the restaurant.

A soft romantic glow seemed to encircle the

round table covered with a white cloth. A small glass vase held a miniature rose. Caleb pulled out her seat and gestured.

"This is very chivalrous of you," Miranda commented after he'd placed a cloth napkin on her lap.

"It's all a part of the plan."

She eyed him suspiciously. "What plan?"

"The one that starts with a little food, a lot of kissing and ends with a nice prelude to baby making."

"Caleb…"

"Look, just kidding. You should loosen up, Ms. Tyler."

Miranda paused as the waiter arrived to pour the water. Glancing around the restaurant, she noticed that the decor was warm and inviting with a fresh, romantic and rustic surrounding. Mahogany wood, rich fabrics and Italian accents gave her a true feeling of dining in a countryside villa. In the background she could hear the barest jingle of pots and pans from the kitchen as opera sang out from invisible speakers.

She sighed. "This is all a little unsettling. Very little has changed in the town since I left home, but I've changed."

Caleb grinned and took his seat. "You've changed for the better. Women age like fine wine. We men are more like moldy cheese. Just ask my mother."

"You are incorrigible."

"It's true. I see it in my patients. Married men are a better grade of cheese than the old bachelors. I might pass that on to your brother."

Miranda laughed out loud, and a warm feeling of affection enveloped him.

God, she's a beauty, Caleb thought. The candlelight flickered and warmed her face as she laughed. Her hair, still disheveled from the wind, curled before her ears and gave him images of it spread out on his pillow. Her skin shone like burnished amber. She looked like she'd been born of his dreams, with her lush lips and dark eyes. How in the world could any man have let her go? How could he have let her go?

"What happened to your marriage, Miranda?"

Sighing, she placed the menu on the table, reached for the water glass and took a sip. "We were good friends."

"I could have guessed that."

"I was struggling with the death of a friend and becoming a single mother. He'd lost his wife in a car accident. It just seemed natural for the two of us to gravitate to one another. He was dependable, good-hearted, charming and honest. I thought maybe the stability he provided would be an answer to my situation."

"It wasn't?"

"No."

"Is that why you divorced?"

"We went into the marriage with the best of intentions and came out of it wiser."

"Did you love him?" Caleb could barely force the words out of his throat.

"I still love him." She paused. "I think of him as a best friend, and he is Kelly's father. But what I feel for him is not the same love my parents share or the kind people sing about. That kind of love is the kind that marriages are based on."

He pondered her response for a moment before saying, "Thank you."

"Why are you thanking me, Caleb?"

He reached across the table and placed his hand on top of hers. Miranda felt the warmth of his regard to the tips of her toes. "For being honest."

She had to look away for the fear of what he would see in her eyes. The ball of apprehension in her stomach grew because fifty percent of what she'd just said had been lies.

"You're welcome. Now are you going to feed me or interrogate me?"

"I'd like to do both and then some. But let me feed you first."

Miranda picked up the menu and pretended to study it. After a few moments, she gave up her pretense, closed the menu and asked, "So what do you recommend?"

"Anything with shrimp."

"Good idea. Let me use my deductive reasoning. The host knows you by name and you have a favorite table, so you're a regular."

"At least twice a week."

"I'm going to guess that you've tried about everything on the menu, except the liver."

"You remember?" He grinned.

"How could I forget the look on your face when my father said that we were having liver for dinner?" Miranda chuckled. "I don't know how you did it, but you managed to eat all of it."

"I didn't have a choice. Your dad practically sat across from me at the dinner table and watched me like a hawk while your brother manipulated me into having to eat a second helping."

"I'm still embarrassed at the way they behaved."

"It was bad, but you know what? I would do it all over again just to see the look of happiness in your eyes."

Miranda ducked her head and looked away. "So what do you recommend?"

Leaning back in the chair, Caleb answered, "I would say that everything on the menu is good, but you might want to try either the lasagna rolls or the spinach fettuccine with chicken and sun-dried tomatoes."

The waiter returned and after they placed their

orders, a comfortable silence settled over the table. A little more than off balance by Caleb's appreciative regard, Miranda asked, "How is your family?"

"Almost all the same. Marius is still a workaholic, Trey has his own veterinary practice in Atlanta, and Regan finally found someone strong enough to take away the keys to her race car and put a ring on her finger."

"Regan's married?" Miranda asked in surprise. If ever there was a poster child for tom girls, Regan was it.

"She just married an artist. I think my mother sent invites to your family. Most likely she was hoping that you would come and put me out of my misery."

"You seem to be very far from miserable."

"Well according to my mother all the unmarried men are miserable, we just ignore it. My uncle James goes out of his way to ignore my mother when she goes into one of her tirades on marriage."

"What is so special about your uncle?"

"He's been a bachelor the longest."

"Is that by choice or circumstance?"

"Both. He made a few bad decisions and ended up losing the woman he loved to another man."

"That's rough."

"For the longest time we all doubted he would ever get into a serious relationship."

"But that's changed?"

"We hope. Last week I heard it through the grapevine that he's bought a place in Atlanta in order to facilitate his hunt for a wife."

Miranda's eyes widened. "You cannot be serious."

Caleb crossed his heart and laughed. "I couldn't be more serious. Apparently, his best friend is tying the knot in Aruba this summer and Uncle James doesn't want to be the last man standing."

"That's a good reason to get married."

"Right now we'll take whatever we can get. The family's still in shock that he's even thinking about a long-term relationship."

Just then the waiter returned with their order. Miranda sat back as the waiter came with their food. "Signora and Signore, *buon appetito.*"

Miranda bowed her head and mentally blessed the food before returning her attention to the handsome doctor across the table.

She had just taken a bite of her spinach fettuccini when he spoke. "So tell me about D.C. How do you like your job?"

"Caleb, I have just taken a taste of manna from the heavens. If you have any mercy, please wait until at least my third bite."

Caleb let out such a laugh that many of the patrons in the restaurant turned toward their table. The men glanced and turned away, but the women's eyes slowly lingered before returning to their meal. When Caleb laughed, it made you forget yourself in the sound.

"D.C. is just a big city with an oversize population of journalists and politicians. I like my job. It has its good days and its bad."

"Would you ever consider moving?"

She eyed him curiously. "Where else would I go?"

"I was thinking more about you coming home...permanently."

Miranda dropped her eyes to her plate and absently stared at her fork. His question wasn't a new one. Her family had been asking for years. And recently she'd been wondering the same thing herself. She had friends in Washington and a good life, but something had always seemed to be missing. Since she'd been home, she hadn't felt that way.

Oh, dear Lord, it felt so right. She was enjoying the meal and the conversation. She also enjoyed hearing his voice and the look of tender amusement in his eyes as they talked.

Miranda couldn't help but recall their first real date when he'd picked her up from her dorm and taken her to a small Indian restaurant.

"Can I ask you a question, Caleb?"

"You can ask me anything, beautiful."

"What made you decide to become a doctor?"

His eyes had widened in surprise—and she'd lain in bed that night wondering what he'd expected her to ask. Maybe questions about his family, his wealth, his reputation as a ladies man.

"I guess it's more of a *when* than *why.*"

"How so?"

"In high school, I'd planned on majoring in finance and working alongside my brother at the company."

"Why did you change?"

"One of my good friends had a severe seizure during class one afternoon." Caleb took a sip of water. "My classmates and I sat there watching until the ambulance came. I didn't like the feeling of complete helplessness. It just became more evident in college that I was much better at being a doctor than a number cruncher."

And she remembered their first kiss in the front seat of his car.

Sweet Jesus, his kiss had felt good. His kiss, his mouth was hot and firm, yet tender lips. They had moved over hers with gentle gliding motions. His cologne mingled with the scent of leather. He'd settled his lips on the corner of her mouth and teased her bottom lip with his teeth.

"Miranda?"

She blinked and her mind cleared of memories. "I'm sorry, can you repeat what you just said?"

"I'd rather know about the thoughts that are making your cheeks flush."

Gathering together a semblance of calm, she met those brown eyes and her skin tingled. She picked up the napkin, patted her lips and then replied, "I was remembering our first date."

"It was one of the best nights of my life."

"I thought that was the night that we saw Alvin Ailey." She smiled.

"I said *one of,* not *the best.*"

Miranda looked away and for the next hour they talked about everything from music to politics. They debated why the Canadian health-care system wouldn't work in America and what it would take for Medicare to succeed. They also had a lively discussion about the effects of television on the youth, and that they didn't produce programs like *The Cosby Show* anymore.

"So what is it that you do again?" Caleb asked.

"I work for the Justice Department's Witness Protection Agency. It's more of the 'behind the scenes' support. Federal Marshals do a lot of the work. I just assist with the background stuff."

"You're the details woman?" he said.

"Exactly."

"It really fits with your personality. Helping the good guys and putting the bad guys behind bars. You save lives just like me."

She chewed her lip for a moment as her mind

processed Caleb's observation. Miranda felt a moment of discomfort as Caleb's assessing gaze grew all the more intent.

"So, as a person who is an expert on hiding people, I bet you'd be good at finding someone."

"I never thought about it that way, but I guess it would be the same, just in reverse."

As they returned to their meal, a mother and child were seated at a table alongside theirs. The little girl looked to be about a year old. She was taken with Caleb. She waved her rattle and cooed all the while those brown eyes watched Miranda's lunch companion like a hawk.

Smiling at Caleb, Miranda commented, "I think she's in love."

"Who?" He looked up from his meal. She pointed to the little baby in the stroller. Caleb looked over, waved at the little girl and chuckled as the baby began to wave her rattle vigorously.

Caleb smiled, finishing his lunch. "I wish I could attract the attention of a certain beautiful project manager the same way I get attention from the under-one-year-old females."

Throughout the meal, he'd watched her under the guise of eating. His pasta could have turned to sawdust for as much as he paid attention to the taste of his own meal. He'd thoroughly enjoyed watching her mouth as she ate her pasta. And the sight of her lips as she sucked in a string of fettuccine had taken the sensuality of Italian food to another level.

"Well, I hear that most men like them young and the women love them old."

"Ouch." He grinned and clutched at his chest in imagined pain.

"I'm curious, Caleb. Are you seeing someone? And why hasn't some handpicked southern belle put a ring around your finger?"

His response was cut off by the waiter's arrival with coffee. The answer when it came was surprising in its honesty. Caleb added cream and sugar to his cup. "Fear," he said.

"How so?"

He looked at her with serious eyes. "Fear of waking up and realizing that I'd made a mistake. And the fear of a lifetime of regret for not being man enough to come after you."

Temporarily rendered speechless, Miranda looked down at her coffee and groped for some witty or sarcastic remark to make light of his statement. But the harder she tried, the less she could think of a response.

"Look, Caleb…" she started.

Seeing her nervously chewing on the edge of her bottom lip, Caleb felt a protective pang in his heart. "Miranda, I didn't say that to force you to respond. I just wanted to be honest and put my cards out on the table. If it hadn't been for my actions, we could have been married with our own house full of kids. I believe that with every fiber of my being, and I'm warning you now that I'm not going to let this opportunity pass by."

Miranda's brow arched while her gaze filled with curiosity. "And if I disagree?" she asked softly.

"Do you?"

She inhaled deeply. "I don't know. I think…"

"Tell me how you feel first." His voice deepened and compelled Miranda to answer as he stared across at her. And for a moment, the attraction flared between them.

Miranda shook her head to try and pull herself out of the enticing spell he seemed to weave. "Confused, frustrated, scared."

Their eyes collided. "You can be all those things, but you have to know that I would never purposefully hurt you."

They sipped their coffee in the silence and afterwards made their way back to the hospital. Ever the perfect gentleman, he kept up a stream of small talk all the way.

Upon pulling into his designated parking space, Caleb turned off the engine but kept the stereo on. He reached over and turned down the volume. "You're not upset about lunch, are you?"

Miranda shook her head and inhaled deeply. The second the warm tantalizing scent of his cologne hit her nose she regretted it as she felt her nipples harden.

She looked over at him. "I could lie."

"You don't have to."

"I've missed you, Caleb," she confessed. "I've had so many sleepless nights and regrets and dreams. I so wanted for you to be the one. The one my grandmother told me would come into my life and everything would be all right. And for those short years, it happened. But like a fairy tale, it ended. And I can't go through that again. I don't think I can handle it."

He leaned toward her and trailed his fingertips over the soft curve of her cheek. "Maybe you can't," he said softly, "but I can. I'll handle it for both of us."

Her eyes dropped down and she nibbled on her bottom lip. If he didn't have to sign Darren's discharge papers and afternoon patients to see, Caleb could have taken advantage of the enticing view and kissed all of her doubts away. Inhaling deeply, he fought down the urge to take her mouth and instead took her hand and squeezed.

"We could be making a mistake, Caleb," Miranda warned as a last-ditch effort to get him to change his mind.

"Warning duly noted. Now how about you grab your brother while I see some sick patients?" He impulsively leaned close to unfasten her seat belt and

Miranda almost fell out of the SUV trying to avoid him.

"Relax, Miranda. I'm not going to kiss you… unless you want me to?"

"In your dreams."

"Actually…" he started.

She put a hand over his lips. "Never mind, I don't want to know."

Miranda tried to move away, but couldn't as he grabbed hold of the safety belt. This was exactly the kind of close physical contact she didn't need while being with him. It reminded her of the reasons she'd had to put hundreds of miles between them and why she'd given her mirror image a pep talk beforehand.

"Look, Caleb. If we're going to be seeing each other on a regular basis, I want to set a few ground rules."

"Ground rules? I distinctly remember you, Miranda Tyler, being the best rule breaker in the entire women's dorm."

Refusing to blush at the accuracy of his statement, she drew in a deep breath. "The new rules are as follows—no flirting, no kissing, no teasing, no brushing your fingertips across my cheek, no holding hands, no whispering in my ear, or telling me I'm beautiful."

"So I can't tell the truth, either." He looked her over from head to toe and Miranda had a hot flash.

"None of that, either," she whispered.

"What did I do?"

"Don't give me that innocent look, Caleb," Miranda said, irritation evident in her voice. "It only worked once. I don't want you looking at me like you've seen me naked."

"I have seen you naked, and I am trying to see heaven every day for the rest of my life."

"If you don't stop, this deal is over. You can find another patient."

"What about your brother?"

"I can't see Darren getting all broken up if you decided to remove yourself from his case. Now do we have a deal?"

He let out what she could only describe as a growl. "This is going to be hell."

"That's all up to you," Miranda pointed out, giving him a serious look.

"Because you're afraid to get involved with me again?"

"Correction, I'm wise enough not to get mixed up with you again."

"Wisdom has nothing to do with fear. I promise that I will never hurt you, if you give me a chance."

"I don't need your promise because I can't give you a chance, Caleb. Now can you stick to the agreement?"

"Do I have a choice?"

"You always have a choice."

"And if I choose to follow my heart?"

"More like your libido. And if you make that choice, you're going to have to find yourself another patient," she warned.

"All right, you win." He paused. "For now…"

Miranda let loose a breath she hadn't realized she'd been holding. She'd needed him to agree to her terms more than she would have ever admitted. His comments had hit far too close to home. It hadn't taken her long to recall all the things she loved about Caleb, nor had it taken her body long to recall all the wonderful sensations he could coax from her body. In asking him to agree to her rules, she'd bluffed Caleb and won.

"Don't want to be late for your brother's discharge, do we?"

An hour later, after getting home from the hospital and helping her brother settle into his old room in their parents' house, Miranda was still distracted by Caleb's behavior. It was only Kelly's arrival back from school that shocked her back to the present.

Yet, later on that night after everyone was settled into bed, Miranda allowed herself to hope.

Maybe this time things would go her way.

Her cell phone rang and her heart gave a little thump as Caleb's name flashed up on the caller ID.

"Hello?"

"Did I catch you before you went to sleep?"

Miranda sat up in bed and switched the phone to the other ear. "I was awake."

"I enjoyed having lunch with you today. So much so that I forgot to tell you about that project I'd like your help with."

"You've told me before that I've rendered you speechless. Are you telling me that I'm taking your memory as well?"

"You could be, little one. I know that when you're near me I can't seem to think of anything else."

"Okay, enough of the flattery, Blackfox."

"Do you know that you only call me by my last name when you're blushing? Are you blushing now, Miranda?"

Heat warmed her cheeks, but she'd be damned if he'd know it. "No," she said quickly.

"Liar."

"Was there a reason you called me in the middle of the night?" she questioned, needing to turn the topic of conversation to safer waters. "I'm sure you called for a better reason than to call me a liar, Caleb."

"True. Before I ask for your help, can I tell you a story?"

"Does this story have a happy ending?" she asked, settling down in the bed.

"Maybe. That depends on you."

"I'm intrigued."

"Good. Close your eyes."

Miranda did as he asked and her body went hot at the intimacy of hearing his deep voice in her ear.

"My great-grandfather Abraham Blackfox was an ex-slave and a mechanical genius. A very simple man, all he ever needed existed in a converted barn on the former plantation where he'd lived most of his young life as a companion to the owner's son, Collin Archer. The only time Collin ever left town was when he went to Philadelphia to collect a wife who had been chosen by his relatives. When Collin went to Philadelphia he took Abraham with him.

"No one knew the real reason why Collin took my great-grandfather with him. Some say to make sure he returned, others said he came as a friend and with the express purpose of keeping Abraham from being arrested by the sheriff who wanted to keep the former slaves from leaving Georgia. One thing that we do know is that something had changed. My great-grandfather received a clear deed to the land my parents' house sits on today, and moved off the plantation. Nine months after he married, his wife, Rebecca, bore Lucas Blackfox, a boy child who had distinct Archer facial features and green eyes. My great-grandfather continued to work in the converted barn and went on to invent many of the precursors to carpet mill machines still used today. And he did it all for the man who'd betrayed him and for the family which had once owned him.

"In my great-grandfather's generation, Collin Archer was one of, if not the wealthiest man in the southeast. His carpet products were shipped around the world. When he died, Collin left fifty percent of the company to Abraham Blackfox. The inheritance didn't appease my grandfather. He blamed Collin Archer for his older brother Lucas's disappearance and hated that the man's actions had unrightfully made him to be second in a time when the firstborn son inherited. So he negotiated with the Archers and struck a deal that led to the creation of Blackfox Trucking. My grandfather traded most of his stock in Archer Carpet for the money to buy a fleet of trucks and exclusive shipping rights to Archer Industries."

At the pause in his voice, Miranda spoke up. "This is a sad story, Caleb."

"It's not over yet. To this day Blackfox and Archer work together, attending meetings, and sit on the same community board, but never speak. My cousin Savannah is engaged and pregnant by Jack Archer and my grandfather would like nothing better than to throw him in jail while the other half of the family wants to brainwash her into leaving him."

"I met your cousin at Kelly's school. She's sweet."

"We all think that, which is why I'm trying to help her."

"I feel bad for your family troubles." Miranda squelched a yawn. "But what does this have to do with me?"

"My hope is that by reuniting my grandfather with his older brother, Lucas, we can start the healing process between our families. And you, Miranda, are the only one that can find him."

Chapter 9

Caleb finished writing out a prescription, tore it from the pad and held it out to his patient's wife. "Give him plenty of fluids, rest and this prescription to lower his blood pressure and he should be fine in a couple of days. If not, make sure to call me or bring him back to the clinic."

"Everybody at the lodge didn't have no problem with the little blue pill, doc. Why me? Just spice things up in the bedroom, you know?"

"If you want to spice things up in the bedroom, how about burning a candle or two, maybe picking up your socks?" his wife responded. "Just turning off the television would definitely get me in the mood. How can a wife feel sexy when you're shouting at those overgrown boys on the basketball court?"

Caleb shook his head and struggled with the urge to grin. This had to have been his third case this week. The little blue pills floating around in the marketplace these days had men thinking they were either supermen or having a heart attack.

"You might want to listen to your wife on this one, Mr. Baker. Viagra is a prescription medication and as you felt this morning, it can have some nasty side effects."

"Thank you so much for taking care of him, Dr. Blackfox."

He nodded. "The hospital pharmacy down the hall can fill your prescription. Remember to give me a call if you have any questions."

As the husband dressed, Caleb departed and made his way back to his office in the main building. Once there, he took a seat behind his desk and put his feet up. It had been a busy morning filled with chest pains, stitches, high fevers and other ailments. It was the time of the season. Any day now the second wave of influenza and bronchitis cases would come into the emergency room, and until then he would spend the bulk of his day assisting at the hospital's free clinic.

Deciding to take a few minutes to himself, he twirled around in his chair and logged on to his computer. While he waited for all of his patient files for the afternoon to load, he leaned back in his chair thinking about Miranda.

Last night he'd told her about one of the most sensitive parts of his family history. Although everyone in town knew about the Blackfox family, not many knew the origin for the tension with the Archers. Switching over to his e-mail account, he clicked through the messages until he came to one from Gill.

Per your brother's request, I have attached all of the information the private investigators could find related to Lucas Evans Blackfox.

Moving his keyboard closer, he quickly typed in a forwarding e-mail address. By the time he had sent the message, another idea popped into his head.

Ten minutes later he hung up the phone, then leaned back in this chair and folded his arms behind his head with a grin.

Hearing a light tap on the door, he glanced up to see his friend and fellow colleague standing in the doorway. Grace Samson had been appropriately named, Caleb thought, as she gracefully handled her patients' recovery and rehabilitation.

"Got a minute to talk?" she asked.

He glanced at his watch and nodded. According to his schedule, he had a little under half an hour before his next appointment. "Yes, come on in."

Grace took a seat in the chair and let out a big yawn. "Sorry, I didn't get much sleep last night."

Leaning forward, Caleb rested his elbows on the desk and smiled. "Missing our cantankerous patient already?"

"Funny, Blackfox. I accidentally volunteered to be on call for the high school football championship. Little did I know that the game would go into like triple overtime and on the ride back the bus got a flat tire. I didn't see my pillow until about four o'clock this morning."

"I know how you feel."

"Speaking about our mutual patient, how did his discharge go yesterday?"

"Contrary to his sister's belief, I think Darren wasn't all that eager to leave. I took Miranda to a two-hour lunch, and Darren had somehow managed to stall his exit for another hour. I honestly think he was waiting for you to walk through the door."

"I told him that I wouldn't be here to kick him out of the hospital."

"Guess he didn't believe you."

She looked genuinely happy at Caleb's response. He shook his head. "I don't believe it. How does a domineering, stubborn, chauvinistic guy like Darren Tyler get a woman like you to fall for him?"

Grace paused and a frown graced her lips for a moment before she sighed. "The same way you convinced him to take you on as his doctor and got his little sister to go out with you."

"He's definitely not as good looking." Caleb laughed.

"But he's just as manipulative," she countered.

Caleb drew in a sigh and rubbed his chin. She was right. He wanted to find his great-uncle just as much as his older brother. But the main reason he'd asked for Miranda's help was not because he knew she could succeed, but it would be an excuse for him to spend more time with her and Kelly.

"So what has he gotten you to do?"

Her eyes widened with surprise and then she shook her head. "In-home rehabilitative therapy."

Caleb laughed until his eyes watered. The irony of the situation couldn't have been more apparent. While he was trying his best to carve out a place in the Tyler family, Grace had been given an all-season pass.

"Do you even offer that service?"

Grace sighed again. "Technically? No. I don't know what I was thinking."

Caleb's eyes filled with laughter. "And that's why you're in my office."

Grace crossed her legs, sat forward and cradled her chin in her hand. "He's a patient, Caleb. You know the rules—we shouldn't get involved with our patients."

"Grace, he's really not your patient—he's mine. And I think that having you around is the best therapy the man can get. He's practically chomping at the bit to endure weeks of pain."

"Be serious."

"I am. I'm going to let you in on a little secret about Darren Tyler. He's tough on the outside, but a marshmallow on the inside."

"So you're saying that he's all bark and no bite?"

"He'll bite you, but he won't be biting me. It doesn't take a medical degree to see the chemistry between the two of you. Just see where it goes."

He hit the print key and reached over to grab the documents from the printer.

They both stood at the same time and Grace smiled at him. "I might just do that."

Caleb reached for his stethoscope and draped it around his neck, then walked beside Grace down the hospital corridor. "And if you should decide to stop by at around five o'clock this evening, you should find your new patient conveniently home alone."

She aimed a suspicious glance his way. "How are you going to get Miranda and Kelly out of the house without her protective older brother following you?"

"Oh, I plan to take the girls out to the one place I know Darren will not want to go."

"And where on earth would that be?"

"106 Ashberry Avenue," he declared smugly.

She came to a dead stop and Caleb did the same. "You aren't."

"Oh, yes. The Tyler women and I are going skating tonight."

Grace laughed and Caleb joined in. His heart lighter than it had been in years. His girl was back and he was going to show her a good time.

Miranda was awakened by the booming sound of a neighborhood teenager's amplified stereo driving past the front of the house. The sun had already risen, and it had been a chilly night but her sheets were damp with moisture.

She squeezed her eyes shut and groaned in frustration. It was Saturday morning, the only time that she was allowed to sleep in and the vehicle had managed to ruin the best part of her dream. For most of her adult life, Miranda had never been able to recall her dreams, but somehow since coming home, she could remember them with almost high-definition clarity. In fact, she vividly remembered most if not all of her dreams for the past two weeks. Last night, she'd covered half the positions in the *Kama Sutra* while making love to Caleb.

Rolling onto her side, she stared at the closed curtains while waiting for her heart rate to slow and the sexual tension in her body to dissipate. After managing to remain celibate for three years, why all of a sudden did her hormones kick into overdrive?

Who are you kidding? A sigh escaped her lips. The dreams and the X-rated fantasies could only be attributed to Caleb. He was the only man who'd ever made her pass out from the sheer ecstasy of his lovemaking. Just the thought made her shiver. His late-night phone call hadn't helped her keep her emotional distance, either. Long after she'd agreed to help locate his missing uncle, she'd stared at the ceiling. Could she find him?

It made her more than a little uncomfortable looking for someone who so obviously didn't want to be found. It was her job to help people start over. Could she just as easily do the opposite? She had the resources and she'd had to do it before to triple check that the high-profile witness protection members could not be tracked down. It would take a few days and she would have to call in a few favors, but she would do it. She would find his great-uncle and return the favor. Nothing personal; Miranda Tyler repaid her debts.

Right, the sarcastic voice in the back of her mind taunted.

Miranda closed her eyes momentarily, giving in to the temptation to linger in the memory of their last kiss. But the sound of her brother hobbling down the hallway reminded her that she had a long list of errands and tasks to accomplish that day.

Pushing thoughts of Caleb from her head, she rose from the bed, strolled over to the window and peeked out. The newspaper had already been delivered. Taking note of the increasingly cloudy sky, Miranda made a mental note to find her gloves as she pulled on her robe. After rummaging through her dresser for a fresh set of underwear and a change of clothing, she tiptoed down the hallway to the bathroom. A few minutes after brushing her teeth and pulling back her hair, she stood underneath the spray of hot water. Her nipples hardened and her belly tightened as she recalled part of a dream where she and Caleb had shared a steamy shower.

As much as she tried to deny it, she knew she'd never be fully over the man. When it was time for her to return to D.C., she wouldn't be able to go without leaving a bigger piece of her heart in his hands. Even if she didn't give in to the old feelings, the new ones would make leaving tough.

She finished her shower, turned off the water and wrapped herself in a towel. Ten minutes to the second, she emerged from the bathroom dressed and ready to go. She was just in time to move away and see a half-asleep Kelly stumble from her room into the hallway.

"I was going to run to the grocery store. Want me to wait for you?" Miranda asked, although she knew the answer. On the cusp of being a teenager, the grocery store was the last place the girl would want to go on a Saturday morning. Had she but mentioned the possibility of going to the library, electronics store, or a bookstore, Kelly would have broken her neck getting ready to go.

"Your brother ate my cereal," she grumbled sleepily.

Miranda smiled at the statement. *Your brother.* Whenever Darren did something that Kelly liked, he was Uncle D. When he did something horrible, he was Miranda's brother.

"Okay, I'll get one box for him and another for you."

"And orange juice, too, please."

Miranda bent down and gave Kelly a quick hug.

"What was that for?"

"For being such a wonderful kid," Miranda answered seriously. "You've been through more traumas in your short life than adults twice my age. You are truly amazing."

"No." Kelly shook her head. "Daddy's amazing. He's always been there for me, especially after Mom died. Even now I know that he's pushing hard so that he can come get me."

The child's bright smile dimmed a little.

"What's wrong?"

"Is it true that when the trial is over I won't get to go home?"

Miranda nodded her head. "You can't go back, but you get to make new friends and make a new home with your dad." She tried to put a positive spin on the situation.

"Does that include you and Uncle D?"

Her heart sank and for a millisecond Miranda wished Kelly wasn't so perceptive. Unwilling to give the child more bad news, she lied. "Of course not. One of the perks of working with your dad is that I get to continue contact with the people in the agency. We may not see each other often, but we can keep in touch."

"So there's no chance that you could come with us? Maybe be my mom for real?"

"Oh, honey." Miranda bent down and wrapped her arms around Kelly. Her eyes began to tear up.

"You do like my dad, don't you?"

"Of course I like your dad."

"But not as much as you like Dr. Blackfox," Kelly surmised.

Miranda inhaled and exhaled slowly. Over five months ago, she and Ryan had gone out on something close to being a date. He was kind, handsome, responsible, a loving father and an awesome agent. They got along well and she trusted him implicitly, but there hadn't been chemistry. No sparks or hot flashes. Her lips didn't tingle from his kiss nor did her skin ache for his touch as it did with Caleb.

Not willing to give voice to her feelings, Miranda patted Kelly on the shoulder. "Are you sure you don't want to run to the grocery store with me?"

Kelly's mouth opened in a gigantic yawn. "No way. I'm going back to bed."

"Lazy bones. I'll be right back, in case Darren asks."

Feeling slightly more upbeat, she walked back to her bedroom to pick up her coat and purse.

Five minutes later, Miranda was in her parents' car heading south on Route 112. Lucky for her, the parking lot was almost completely empty. She pulled into the first vacant space, climbed out of the car and quickly crossed the parking lot. The icy wind made her eyes tear as she pulled out a shopping cart. Once inside, she took her time wandering up and down the aisles, picking out fresh fruit and picking up whatever looked good. Only after she'd gotten halfway through the store and her cart was close to overflowing did Miranda realize that she didn't have a list.

She stopped dead in the middle of the store and chuckled to herself. Any of the grocery store employees watching her at the moment would have sworn she was crazy.

Far from being like her mother and brother,

Miranda had never been organized. Where Darren had an almost military precision to making his bed, she'd been happy if the sheets weren't on the floor. It was only after breaking up with Caleb and moving to Washington, D.C., that things changed. Her therapist had mentioned early on in their sessions that her newly discovered penchant for lists, planning and organization was in response to her feeling powerless. Whatever the case, she honestly could not remember the last time she'd gone grocery shopping without a list.

Pushing the cart down the frozen-food aisle, she came to a stop. Five minutes later she was still standing in the same spot, agonizing over which ice cream really needed to come home with her. After staring at a few of her favorite half-gallon containers for a while, she reached in and took them all.

Ice cream could be a substitute for sex, she mused.

Her waistline might not like it, but her taste buds would be in heaven. The morning air was still cool and crisp, yet her cheeks warmed as she recalled how she had enjoyed her dreams of Caleb. But not near as much as she enjoyed the real thing. In such a short time she had come to realize that there was so much more to the man she'd fallen in love with close to a decade ago. Caleb Blackfox was a handsome, fun-loving, compassionate and dedicated doctor, and any woman would give up her last penny to be with him.

But he wants you.

She shook her head and Miranda was still chuckling to herself as she loaded the bags of groceries into the trunk.

Chapter 10

The doorbell rang on Friday evening just after Miranda had put away the last dish. Drying off her hands, she moved through the house and glanced through the peephole. At the sight of Caleb staring back at her, Miranda's heart skipped a beat.

"Caleb, this is an unexpected surprise."

"Have you missed me?" His deep voice passed over her skin like a feather that left a trail of shivers up and down her spine.

"Of course not." She tilted her chin upward and smiled.

"Good, because I've missed you, too." He

leaned over and gave her a kiss. "Now go change into some jeans. We've got reservations."

"Reservations?" she echoed.

"I'm taking my two favorite girls roller-skating and out to dinner."

"Did you just say roller-skating?" Kelly squeaked.

Miranda turned toward her and opened her mouth to deny it, but the look of pure excitement on the girl's face stopped her cold.

"Yep." Caleb took a few steps into the house. "Want to come?"

"Yeah," Kelly said matter-of-factly.

"Then you'd better grab some socks and shoes."

"What about my brother?" Miranda interjected, trying to pump the brakes.

"He won't miss us."

"And how would you know that?"

"I have it on good authority that a certain physical therapist will be stopping by the house in…" He checked his watch. "Approximately twenty minutes to check on your brother."

"You mean Grace is actually going to ask him out?"

"You knew?"

Miranda smiled smugly. "Of course."

"Then you'd better grab your stuff." He came in and closed the door behind him. "The last thing you want to do is hinder your brother's recovery."

She threw her hands up and turned her back to him. Caleb couldn't help but grin as he suppressed a chuckle. Looking downward at her shapely hips as she stomped away, he allowed himself a moment of pride. For the first time since she'd come home, he'd left Miranda Tyler speechless.

A half hour later, after arriving at the local roller-skating rink, Caleb was inwardly congratulating himself.

He picked up the two pairs of rental skates and ushered them both over to a slightly secluded area away from most of the roller rink's teenage populace. Kelly had already laced on her skates and was ready to go out.

"Can I go skate now? Mindy and Chelsea are here."

Miranda nodded. "All right, but stay close to your friends."

"Will do."

"We'll be watching you, okay?"

Kelly turned on one leg and rushed out onto the skating floor.

"She's pretty fearless," Caleb commented standing beside her.

Pride evident in her voice, Miranda replied, "She's willing to try anything once. She almost gave me a heart attack last Saturday."

"What happened?"

"Kelly decided to experiment by cooking Darren and I breakfast."

Darren's brow furrowed with confusion. "That sounds pretty harmless."

"You don't boil eggs in the microwave," she added.

He laughed, and in unison they drew deep breaths as Kelly turned and began to skate backward.

"Were we ever that fearless?" Miranda asked rhetorically.

"Worse," Caleb answered. "You jumped into the ocean without really knowing how to swim."

"Well you jumped in to save me without a life jacket."

They laughed again and then took a seat. "This isn't going to be that bad. We're just going to be roller-skating."

"Do you have a cell phone close?" Miranda asked.

"Always, but the hospital knows not to call unless it's an emergency."

He'd set out to create just the right opportunity for her to not only see that he could be a good father figure to Kelly, but also a good friend to Miranda. Not to mention Caleb relished the opportunity to touch her.

Called SkatePlex, the facility opened last year. Roller-skating, roller hockey and indoor soccer were available on the bigger-than-normal rink that spanned about 20,000 square feet and could handle more than 200 skaters at one time.

"Dire emergency," he added.

She took off her coat and sat down on the soft bench. "I wasn't worried about your parents. I just want to make sure you'd be able to dial 911 when I wipe out."

"Such confidence." He grinned. Caleb's sarcasm came through clear as a bell over the fast-paced music playing over the speaker system.

Her eyes darted toward the rink and he glimpsed a shadow of fear.

"Caleb, why don't you go out and skate with Kelly? I'll just watch."

Ignoring her comment, he bent down to his knees and pulled off her loafers.

"What are you doing?" she asked.

"Putting on your skates," he answered.

"Why don't you put yours on first?"

"Because it's easier to do this for you first."

"I'd rather you didn't. Really, Caleb. Don't worry about me. I'll be out soon."

"You can't fool me, Miranda." Mirth tickled in his throat at the obvious ploy to get out of skating. Instead, he caught her foot, curled his fingers and started to tickle her instep.

"Caleb! Stop!" she shouted. "You know I'm ticklish down there."

His gaze heated and his body warmed with memories. He knew all of her sensitive spots and loved to play with them. Especially the soft spots under her thighs. "Stop fighting me and I'll quit."

"Okay." She sat back and her shoulders slumped in defeat.

"Good girl."

"You are so bad."

"If you don't behave, I'll get even worse."

He felt like a teenager again, only better. This time he hadn't come with his boys and stood on the corner playing cool and eyeing the girls as they moved around the rink. This time he would have the most beautiful girl on his arm.

"Caleb, you know I haven't been on skates since I was in elementary school."

"So that's how I missed you in high school. My brothers and I would come here almost every weekend and look at the pretty girls. They say skating is just like riding a bike."

She gave him an incredulous look and he laughed out loud.

"Momma, Dr. Caleb. Are you coming?" Kelly shouted from the edge of the rink.

Caleb grinned broadly and waved her over. "Your mother has some crazy idea that she's not going to skate with us."

Kelly's brown eyes were superbright with excitement and the glow on her face warmed Miranda's heart. It was such a blessing to have her this past month. Even her brother had fallen in love with the little girl. And even though Miranda knew that the charade would end once Ryan testified, the sadness brought by the thought of Kelly disappearing from her life was erased by the joy of caring for her.

Kelly pitched herself down on the bench beside Miranda and took her hand. "Don't worry, Dr. Caleb and I will be with you every step of the way."

Miranda gave her a little squeeze and looked up. Caleb had taken a seat on the bench directly opposite theirs and he'd begun to lace up his own roller skates. Assured for the moment that her life wasn't in jeopardy, she turned her attention to Caleb. This was the first time she'd seen him dressed down. He had on Nike sneakers, blue jeans and a burgundy turtleneck sweater that clung to his muscles and emphasized a nice set of shoulders.

As if he'd overheard her thoughts, he looked up and their eyes collided. "That's right, Miranda. Every step of the way."

The double entendre in his tone flew over Kelly's head, but Miranda caught it and she didn't resist the urge to let out a rude snort. "Just remember that when we both hit the floor, Blackfox."

Moments later, after Miranda had practiced stutter-stepping on the carpet, she decided it was time to hit the hardwood. Kelly had long since rejoined her classmates and Miranda watched in awe as the girl flew over the rink like an Olympic ice-skater.

"Ready?" Caleb asked.

She gripped his hand like a lifeline. "If I said no would you take me back to the bench?"

"Not on your life, sweetheart. I've been trying to get you in my arms for weeks now and I'm not giving up this opportunity."

"What if I promise you a kiss?"

"Can I get immediate payment?"

Miranda shook her head. Rome was a small Georgia town. Their being together at the skating rink was bound to get around in no time. Her kissing the daylights out of one of the scions of the Blackfox family would put them both in the top section of the local gossip column.

"Not gonna happen."

"All right then, I'm going to be right by your side like I've been imagining since I woke up this morning."

"So you admit that you've been dreaming about my death?"

He grinned wickedly. "Did you know that the French call the act of climax, *la petite morte*— little death?"

Heat burned in her cheeks and for the moment Miranda was devoid of speech.

Caleb took advantage and moved them forward. "Here we go." He tugged her out onto the floor. Miranda grabbed for his arm and hung on.

They went a few yards before she managed to bark out, "Don't."

"Don't what?"

"Flirt. You're making me nervous."

"I could kiss you. That used to take all your nervousness away when we were dating."

"That would be worse."

"Which would be worse? Would you prefer the kissing or the flirting? I'm going to do one or the other."

"Okay, you can flirt," she responded quickly.

"I'll do whatever it takes to get close to you."

It took a few minutes to complete a circle of the rink and Miranda had almost made it when she wiped out and fell on her rear.

"I thought you were going to be with me every step of the way." She looked up at his laughing face.

He held out a hand and she took it. "I was with you every step of the way. And I'm here to pick you up."

"You should definitely stick to medicine, Caleb. You're a horrible skating instructor."

"But I'm an excellent physician. I'd be more than happy to check out that nice gluteus maximus of yours for bruises."

"Stay away from my behind." Miranda barely managed to keep a straight face at his mock leer.

"Don't fall."

"Fine." She nodded and grabbed a hold of him tightly. "Next time, we're hitting the ground together."

"Ready to start again?"

"If I fall and break my leg, Darren will never forgive you."

"*Darren* won't forgive me? Not *you?*"

"I don't believe in holding a grudge."

"All right then. From now on, beautiful, we're going down together," he promised.

He smiled at Miranda and her already shaken knees grew even weaker. They began to move again and she managed a small wave as Kelly flew by. His body heat warmed her and when he wrapped his arm around her waist, she fit perfectly into his side. As the music slowed and Caleb kept them at a safe pace, Miranda took stock of her situation. No doubt about it, she was in trouble. Not the house-burning-down-around-you-but-with-the-hope-of-finding-an-escape kind of dilemma. More like the trouble in which you sent out a call for help and ran like crazy. Miranda lifted her eyes and met Caleb's chocolate-brown ones and swallowed hard.

* * *

Caleb had just gotten Miranda settled in the concession area when Kelly skidded to a stop beside him.

"I'm thirsty," she announced in a loud breath.

"Good. I was just about to grab us something to drink. You can help me carry them to the table."

"So when can we do this again?" Kelly asked after a minute.

Caleb smiled. "I was going to ask about that. But first, how do you feel about my visiting your mother so much?"

"I'm cool with your dating Ms. Miranda."

Caleb frowned at the way she addressed Miranda but let it go. "And it's okay to take her out?"

"Where to?"

They inched forward in line.

At the thought, Caleb glanced over in Miranda's direction and saw that she was completely at ease. Not that he needed another reason as to why she fascinated him, but being with her today reaffirmed that she was special. Most women were turned on by his profession, the automobiles he drove, and the expensive restaurants he took them to, and simply being seen with Caleb Blackfox, wealthy bachelor about town.

Miranda's expression and attitude told him that she didn't care about his bank account, his house and his social status. He could drive an eighteen wheeler and she'd still care for him.

And so he shrugged before answering Kelly's question. "Dinner, movies, Atlanta. Maybe an overnight trip."

"Do I get to come?"

"Sometimes. There could be other occasions that only grown-ups are allowed."

She tapped her finger against her cheek and he smiled as she seemed to think hard. "I like bowling, Putt-Putt and go-karts," she announced.

Relieved beyond belief, Caleb laughed. "I'll check my schedule."

"She's exhausted," Miranda commented later on as Caleb came to a stop in her parents' driveway.

"I can carry her inside."

"All right," Miranda murmured, checking to make sure she had all their things. "Give me a minute to unlock the door and turn on the lights."

She hopped out of the SUV and made her way to the front door. Before her hand pulled the keys out of her purse, the porch lights flickered on and the door swung open. Momentarily blinded by the light, she blinked.

"About time you decided to come home."

"Were you worried that Caleb had kidnapped us?" she teased before waving toward his SUV.

"No," her brother grumbled before he turned

around and made slow progress toward his bedroom.

The teasing smile disappeared from her lips as she realized that he'd truly been worried. With her brow furrowed, Miranda looked toward the grandfather clock and inhaled with surprise. It was after eleven o'clock.

"Everything okay?"

Miranda jumped at the sound of Caleb's voice beside her. "Fine. I'll show you to her room."

"I can find my way."

"Right." Miranda remembered that Caleb had been in their house just as much as she had.

She moved into the living room and sat on the couch. Closing her eyes, she slipped off her shoes and sighed aloud. She reopened her eyes when she felt the couch shift next to her.

"I think I convinced her to stay awake long enough to change into her pajamas."

"I had fun tonight."

"I'd like to have fun with you every night."

Looking away from his hypnotic gaze, Miranda impulsively asked, "What's the craziest thing you've ever done?"

"Does volunteering to work the late shift in the hospital trauma unit count?"

Miranda shook her head. "Try again."

He put his hands behind his head. "I went skydiving with a group of guys from school."

"Serious?"

He nodded.

"Did you do it in graduate school?"

"No, I did it about a year ago."

"What made you decide to risk your life jumping out of a perfectly good plane?"

"During my residency, I was assigned to the cancer center. I became friends with one of the patients on the floor. He was a young man named David Sutton, but he couldn't have been older than twenty-five. I only knew him for three months before he died."

"How did he die?"

"He had an inoperable brain tumor. You would never have guessed it from the stories he told. David had been around the world and sailed down the Nile River. He showed me pictures of his climb up Mount Kilimanjaro. He swam with the dolphins, ran with the bulls and skydived off the cape of Johannesburg among other things."

"And that made you want to skydive?"

"It was his words before he died. He asked me to remember the story of his life, not his death. He was the first patient I had ever truly known to die in my care."

"That must have hurt." Miranda's voice softened with sympathy.

"As a doctor you're supposed to be able to deal

with the knowledge that someone might not make it. After David's death, I didn't see life around me anymore. All I could see was sickness and death. I wanted to feel alive again. Knowing that I was going through a rough patch, my older brother dared me to jump."

"How did it feel?" she asked, fascinated by the thought of jumping out of a plane.

"Incredibly terrifying and spiritual. I was flying or falling, depending on your point of view. But it answered a lingering question and erased my doubts. I know one thing for sure—you can't jump out of a plane nine thousand feet in the air without faith. Stepping out of that plane was my leap of faith. I learned to trust in God again. I remembered what it felt like to love life."

"That's wonderful, Caleb," Miranda commented.

"I hear a 'but,'" he added.

"There have to be better ways to feel alive than risking your life."

"You're right. Being with you is a lot safer."

Bathed in the soft glow of the lamp, they stared at one another. Mesmerized, she watched as he reached over and placed his fingers on either side of her face...and he kissed her. His lips touched hers lightly, as though asking permission, and then his tongue caressed her lips and slowly entered her mouth.

Caleb's kisses were like the man: slow, intense and calm. She placed her arms around his shoulders and closed her eyes, enjoying the warmth of his kisses and the gentle kneading of his hands on her shoulders. So close to the warmth of his body, Miranda could hear the shallowness of his breath, feel the beating of his heart. Minutes later, when they both came up for air, she knew right then that she wanted to do a lot more than kiss this man. "Now that you've heard my story, what about yours?" he asked.

"I'd have to say that climbing Mount Fuji at night was about the craziest thing I've ever done."

"I almost did that while I was in Tokyo, but I didn't have the time. I passed by Fuji when I took the Shinkansen to Kyoto. How was it?"

"The mountain always looks beautiful from the bullet train. Its white-crusted peak ringed by wispy silver clouds… Being up close is a different story. From bottom to top, Fuji is nothing but a steep mound of rock. I had heard a lot about the mountain but I forgot that it was first and foremost a volcano."

"You climbed at night. Wasn't it dangerous?"

"It was safer than your skydiving adventure. There were a lot of people climbing the night I went. The trail went back and forth on the mountain so I rarely had any vertical climbs. The one thing I will never forget about being on top of Fuji was the stars. The farther up I climbed, the closer they became. Nearing the top, I felt as though I could reach out my hand and touch them. The quiet beauty of the sunrise brought me to tears. Not to mention I was deliriously exhausted by then. I was a mess by the time I got down. Covered in dirt, dust and ash."

"You still would have been beautiful."

Miranda shook her head. "Caleb, I can't…" She started to say something but was cut off by the sound of the phone ringing.

Startled, she drew back and watched as Caleb reached into his pocket and brought out a small flip phone. He looked at her apologetically and answered the phone as it rang again. Miranda sat back and pretended not to listen to the conversation.

"What's her blood pressure? Heart rate? Has her water broken? No. Call me once the water breaks. I'll drop by the hospital on my way home.

"Sorry about that," he said.

"Not a problem. You should go."

"We're not finished."

"Yes, we are."

"Good night, beautiful. I'll see you tomorrow."

Before she could say more, he kissed her on the lips and left.

Chapter 11

"He really likes her, you know."

Darren looked up from his drafting. He moved to rub his neck and winced at the pain. Six weeks. He didn't know if he'd be able to survive that long. The only bright spot would have been his sister's return, but Caleb Blackfox's presence lingered like a rain cloud over everything. Since he'd been released from the hospital, the man came over to the house every day, sometimes twice a day. Then there was Grace.

As much as he loved looking at the beautiful therapist, she acted more like a drill sergeant than a woman. All he wanted to do was put the moves on her, but a broken leg and her nonstop pushing and prodding didn't allow for much romance.

All of his frustrations rose to the surface and he wanted to bite someone's head off. Preferably it would be Caleb Blackfox's. But as long as the doctor threatened to tell Miranda about his part in their breakup, his hands were tied.

Tossing down his mechanical pencil, he turned toward Kelly. "Shouldn't you be doing your homework or something?"

"I finished it up before dinner." She walked into the home office and took a seat on the slip-covered sofa he'd inherited from his parents.

"Dr. Caleb seems like a nice guy."

A muscle in Darren's jaw clenched. Not again. It seemed like everyone in the world had woken up and joined the Caleb Blackfox fan club. Everyone except for him, of course. He didn't care if the man saved lives, volunteered time and donated money to charity. At his core he was a self-centered rich pretty boy who, for the second time, threatened to wreak havoc in his sister's life. Not for the first time, Darren cursed the driver whose inattention had landed him in the hospital. Used to being the one taking care of others, it was depressing that he had to depend on his little sister and the little girl sitting across the room.

"Caleb thinks that he's entitled to have everything he ever wanted, including my sister."

Kelly sat back and crossed her arms under her nonexistent breasts. On a mental level he knew for a fact that Kelly possessed none of his sister's DNA, but at the moment, the little gesture reminded him so much of Miranda he could have sworn she was his true niece.

"I like him," she declared. Her eyes were so full of mischief he had a hard time not smiling.

Darren wanted to say something sarcastic, but he bit his tongue and instead picked up his pencil. If he was going to keep his sister from falling for Caleb, he needed as many allies as possible. "Who do you like more, Caleb or your father?"

"My dad, of course."

"So if you were to choose who Miranda liked more, would it be your dad or Blackfox? I mean isn't it nice having Miranda as a mother?"

Her eyes widened for a second and then slid away. Darren could just imagine the wheels turning inside the girl's head. For a moment his conscience prickled, but he shrugged it away. So he'd just manipulated a child. Not like he'd robbed a bank.

"Well…"

"Miranda and I talk a lot. She's always mentioning how much she enjoyed working with your father. It's not that much of a stretch to take it another step further."

"You hate Dr. Caleb, don't you? What did he

do? Beat you up for lunch money in kinder-garten?"

Darren broke the pencil lead at the comment. Although they had never gone toe-to-toe, there had always been a competitive tension between him and Caleb, especially where the opposite sex was concerned. "I just want what's best for my little sister." He paused. "And if something was to happen and you suddenly became my real niece, I would make sure that Santa Claus deposited some nice presents under your Christmas tree."

Chapter 12

The next few days were the longest in his life. Caleb continued to make his rounds at the hospital, kept follow-up appointments with former patients and gotten caught up with required medical-board reading. He'd even called up a former lady friend and met her for dinner. But he was just going through the motions. Suddenly, life lost its color, the weather turned cold and his mood sank. He'd gone to his own physician, and friend, and gotten a full physical and passed with a clean bill of health. But everything still felt wrong. It wasn't exactly a week after Darren's release from the hospital that he could pinpoint what was wrong with him.

He was lovesick.

It was a terrible feeling made worse because he'd sometimes catch a few stolen kisses when he went over to her house to check up on her brother. Now he had a reason to be glad that they were three time zones apart when they broke up because he couldn't have handled being this close to her. Pushing the thoughts to the back of his mind, he concentrated on the problems at hand.

Normally when the Blackfox boys got together after a family meal, the alcohol flowed along with jokes, wagers and boisterous laughter. There had been many a time when they'd all passed out after too many drinks and a night of fight-watching or pool-playing. Tonight, however, Caleb was still on his first bottle of beer and none of his siblings or cousins seemed to be in a festive mood.

After leaving most of his female relatives upstairs along with the kids, Caleb, his uncle and cousins had ensconced themselves around the circular bar in the finished basement. He'd come downstairs with the express purpose of shooting pool, drinking a beer and keeping his mind off his own personal situation. All he wanted was a few moments without being haunted by the vision of Miranda's thickly lashed dark brown eyes and full lips. Instead he somehow walked into the role of mediator on his cousin's behalf, again.

"Look, everyone, the point is—it's her life."

Caleb banged his hand on the bar and made sure to maintain eye contact with his cousins. "You know that I would be the first to do anything legal or illegal to protect Savannah. But she's not in danger and she doesn't need our help."

"No, she needs psychiatric attention. Caleb, my little sister is about to marry the grandson of the man who almost destroyed our family."

"The key word is *almost* destroyed our family," he parried. Stepping close to Thomas, Caleb placed a hand on his shoulder. "You and I have been going to the same church all of our lives and I know you were awake in Bible study, so you have to remember that the sins of the father don't always have to be visited on the son."

Thomas's face blazed with incredulity. "Marius, are you listening to this?"

Caleb didn't turn to look at his older brother. If he knew Marius, and after living with his older brother for sixteen years during which the man changed his diapers and bought him his first condom, they would agree on the subject of Savannah's impending nuptials and pregnancy.

"I hate to admit it, but Caleb does have a point. Savannah is an adult," Marius stated calmly.

"It *is* Savannah's life," Trey, their younger brother, chimed in. "She should be able to make her own mistakes."

"What?" Thomas stared at them as though he'd

never seen them before. "Would you say the same thing if it were your little sister?"

Trey nodded. "Not a word different."

"Bull." Thomas frowned. "I was there when you threatened to castrate her first boyfriend."

A few chuckles filled the silence in the room; but when Caleb stepped forward to stand alongside his younger brother, everyone managed to put on a straight face.

"Look, cuz. We're here to celebrate Uncle James's birthday and Trey's engagement to Sasha. We don't have to agree with Savannah's choice but we're her family. She's going to need our support and so will our parents. They don't like the situation any more than we do."

"And that's why we have to do something about it."

Frustrated and fed up with saying the same thing over and over, Caleb stepped toward his inebriated cousin. "What are you going to do, Thomas? Lock Savannah in her room? Your parents tried that and did it work? She's pregnant and Jack Archer is about a hairsbreadth from pressing charges against you and David for assault."

Thomas winced, but Caleb didn't feel a bit of sympathy. Luckily he'd still been in the parking lot when they'd called him from the emergency room at the hospital. The last thing their family needed was a renewed feud with the Archer family and the ensuing bad publicity.

"I just don't want her to get hurt," Thomas said honestly.

Famous last words, Caleb thought. He would have rather cut himself than to ever hurt Miranda, but it had happened and he was sure that it would happen again. All he could do was hope that what they built together this time around was strong enough to hold even when they were angry with one another.

Marius finished his drink in one gulp, stood up, and grinned. "Just think about it this way—Jack Archer is marrying into our family. If he screws up, he'll have all of us plus your sister to deal with."

"Yeah." Caleb laughed. "It almost makes me feel sorry for him."

And for the first time since they'd gathered downstairs, the Blackfox boys broke into laughter. Caleb took a seat and pretended interest in the sports wrap-up on the television, but in fact his thoughts returned to Miranda. He couldn't wait to see her again but hated the fact that he couldn't get her alone. It had been three weeks since he'd seen her standing next to Darren's bedside and in that span of time, he could count on his fingers the number of times he'd been able to kiss her. Memories of the brief times he had gotten close enough to touch her, however briefly, made him hotter than a teenager locked in a bathroom with a Victoria's Secret magazine. But the wanting went beyond physical desire. More than ever, he wanted her in his life full time. He wanted to walk into a home instead of an empty house.

A sudden sensation of frustration made his hands curl into fists. He'd been patient, kind, considerate and spent as much time as he could to get to know Kelly. Hell, he'd even been polite to Miranda's older brother who'd taken every opportunity to insult him. Caleb had even gone so far as to say that they were like oil and vinegar. They could be in the same space, but they'd never mix. With his campaign in full gear, how could she resist? Or a better question would be—how did he break down her defenses?

He didn't want to talk to his father or uncles; their advice would be to wait and let her come to him. Blackfox men are the object of female pursuit, not the other way around. They would hold that party line against a mountain of contradictory evidence. He'd witnessed firsthand the number of hoops his father would jump through for every anniversary and Christmas. Dad didn't like dogs, especially small dogs, but he'd given his wife a toy poodle for Christmas. The rumor around the family was that the pedigreed pooch had a plate at the table and slept at the foot of the bed.

Not in the mood to hear another lecture from Marius, he settled on asking the only person left.

Moving away, he tapped his younger brother on the shoulder and motioned him over to a quieter section near the wet bar.

"Trey, I need to ask some advice."

"Wait." His younger brother chuckled. "I need a witness and a drink for this moment."

"Funny. Maybe I should just talk to Uncle Mark." As Trey took a swig of beer, Caleb dragged a weary hand over his brow.

"Wait, I was just kidding. What happened to your sense of humor?"

"I left it in the emergency room on a respirator."

"Wow. Okay, what's up?"

"I need to win someone over. And since everyone loves veterinarians, I thought you'd have some insight."

"Young, old or female? I can help you with the first two, but the last one? Impossible."

"It must not be since you got Sasha to agree to put you out of your misery."

"I see you've got jokes. Guess you really need my help, doctor."

"That's the problem. I thought that if I treated the symptoms, i.e. the leftover mistrust Miranda had from our breakup, that we could pick up where we left off."

"But that's not happening?"

"No. I see her every day, or I try to. And for every step I take forward, she sidesteps twice. When I try to get her alone, something always manages to get in the way."

Caleb rubbed his chin in a show of deep thought. "So to kiss her until she forgets her own name, falls head-over-the-hills in love, and can't live without you won't be an option?"

"Not yet. I'm trying."

"Well, since your human techniques aren't working, let me give you the ultimate in animal wisdom. It's worked for millennia and I'm telling you this because my future wife spilled the secret to me last night."

"Huh?" Caleb's jaw dropped. "Sasha's giving you hints on how to get women?"

"No. She's writing an article on mating habits in the wild for a woman's magazine's Valentine's Day issue. I got to read the rough draft. Sasha's got a gift for writing that you wouldn't believe."

Caleb took a swig of the beer in his hand and struggled not to laugh at the enamored expression on his brother's face. "I'm sure. Now what's the secret?"

"First, take them by surprise. Second, never take no for an answer. Third, find out what they really want, and then hold out to give them what they need."

"That's it?" he questioned. Caleb was sure there had to be more. It couldn't be that simple.

"In a nutshell. I guarantee results."

"Is that a money-back guarantee?"

Trey's eyes twinkled with mirth as he tapped his beer bottle against Caleb's. "Money back? You still owe me money—a couple of grand—from that last trip to Vegas."

"Would you rather I wrote you a check or told your future wife about that really flexible show-girl with the long weave that could have been a spokesmodel for *Video Vixen's* magazine?"

"Just go get the girl, damn it."

Trey's lips clamped tight around the beer bottle, and Caleb threw his head back and roared with laugher. "Will do."

Chapter 13

"Darren, time to get up!"

"What…where's the fire?" he muttered as Miranda continued to shake him.

"There's no fire," she explained. "But you've got to take a shower and get dressed or we're going to be late."

Turning over, he squinted at the clock on the nightstand. The dial read 9:00 a.m. "Why? I'm not going to church."

"You're not going to church? What about dinner at Aunt Pat's?"

"Bring me back a couple of servings."

"Do I look like room service to you?"

"No, you look like my lovely little sister that will be praying for her shut-in older brother at church this morning."

"Aunt Pat's going to be disappointed. You know she's expecting us to be there."

"I already know what she's going to say. 'You need to have your behind in church and not in the bed. Your parents didn't raise heathens.'" Darren's voice was almost an exact replica of their aunt's.

Miranda took a step back and did her best to glare at Darren. But her anger lacked conviction and they both knew it. "You can't just hide in the house until you can walk again."

"Want to bet?"

"It's unhealthy," she pointed out.

"It's safe. The less I move around the better my chances of not messing up the only good leg I have."

"That doesn't make sense."

"Letting Caleb Blackfox back into your life doesn't make sense either, but you don't see me lecturing you about that mistake now do you?"

"That was a low blow."

"Truth hurts." Darren's smug grin had her fingers curling into fists.

"And it's going to leave you hungry." She twirled around on her heels and stomped toward the bedroom door. "Just for that comment, you can kiss your pancakes goodbye."

Let him fend for himself for a little while, she groused. It was way past time the men in her life learned a lesson. "Miranda Tyler is nobody's doormat," she muttered, sticking her hands in the pockets of her robe. With that thought in mind, she headed for the kitchen. She and Kelly were going to have banana pancakes and she'd make sure big brother would have none.

"I said do something unexpected, not ambush the woman at church, Caleb."

Caleb put the SUV in Park before grinning at his younger brother. "What better place to show Miranda and the rest of the town and our family that I'm serious about having Miranda in my life?"

"In your life or as your wife?" Trey asked.

"Both." He flipped the driver's side visor down and took one last look in the mirror. A trip to the barber shop the other morning assured him that his hair was properly shaped and he'd taken extra time to give himself a clean shave that morning.

Trey frowned. "Did you just say something about showing the family?"

Caleb nodded. "I invited Mom, Dad and the rest of the family."

"You are serious, big brother?"

"No, I'm getting desperate. Now let's get inside before they arrive."

After leaving his parents and his brother comfortably situated in sanctuary, Caleb returned to the entrance hall to wait for Miranda. He glanced at his watch, sure that she would be on time. Normally the last thing he expected was for a woman to be on time. But early on in their relationship Miranda had cured him of that prejudice. And exactly fifteen minutes before the service began, the front doors opened and the air whooshed out of his chest.

He'd expected her to look nice, but in truth she was more than that. Beautiful, delicate, maternal and perfect. No other words could describe how she looked as she entered the church holding Kelly's hand. The black pantsuit fit her body like a glove and showcased her legs. To complete the look, a slender string of pearls rested on her elegant neck and matching teardrops adorned her ears. Miranda could entice a man one moment and care for a child the next.

When he heard the rubbing sound of leather, Caleb looked down and realized he was squeezing his Bible. Relaxing his grip, he stepped into Miranda's path.

"Good morning, Sister Tyler and Ms. Kelly."

Miranda's bright pecan-colored eyes widened with shock. They rounded even more so as they watched his head descend and his lips land on her cheek.

She was going to faint. Fall over in the church entranceway, be taken to the hospital and then straight to jail after she killed the man in front of her. Unable to think straight, Miranda wondered if she could just kick him. What would happen to Kelly if Miranda's trial was published all over the country? What would her parents think? And why did the gesture make her body all tight and tingly?

Before she could walk away, Kelly stepped forward to Caleb's waiting arms for a warm hug, and then out of nowhere Miranda was surrounded by members of the church.

She pasted a bright smile on her face and said, "Good morning, Deaconess Smith."

The woman enveloped her in a generous hug, and then beamed. "I'm so happy for you, Miranda. I know your parents are going to be tickled pink when they find out that you and Caleb are back together," she said.

Not wanting to give the wrong impression, Miranda shook her head and interjected, "No, ma'am. Caleb and I are just friends."

Smiling and placing her hand on his arm, Caleb added, "For the moment. I'm wearing down her defenses."

Miranda felt the urge to run, but she really wanted to kill Caleb.

Sorry, Lord. She mentally sent up the apology.

"And what a beautiful daughter you have.

She's got your mother's cheeks. What's her name?"

"Kelly, come over and meet Deaconess Smith. She taught my Sunday school class."

Miranda was so proud when Kelly walked over and gave the woman a hug. In no time, she managed to wrap the elder saint around her little finger.

Feeling a hand at the center of her back, Miranda turned her head and through gritted teeth she whispered, "What's wrong with you?" Only to be rewarded by a broad grin and a suggestive wink.

"What are you doing here?" She pushed out the sentence, and then cleared her throat when she realized that she sounded like a hissing snake.

"Escorting two of the most beautiful girls in Georgia to church. Ready to go in?"

Miranda blinked helplessly as Kelly took Caleb's hand and they both stood there looking at her with expectant looks on their faces. Her eyes darted to the other church members. And the senior saints she recognized from her childhood stood watching their little group with unabashed interest.

She turned back to Caleb and the grin on his face hadn't slipped an inch. He had her just where he wanted her and she'd never seen this move coming.

When the time came to enter the church, she

wanted to run. Miranda felt as though the entire congregation was staring at their little party as they walked down the aisle. She passed her aunt and uncle and watched as Aunt Pat did a double take upon seeing her with Caleb. Uncle Allan, on the other hand, appeared as though nothing out of the ordinary had occurred.

"You are so wrong, Caleb Blackfox." She spoke out of the side of her mouth, but somehow managed to keep a smile on her face in order to cover her mortification. Caleb had escorted them down the center of the aisle to almost the very front of the sanctuary.

"One of the deacons insisted that my family sit in front."

Miranda almost tripped. "Your family?"

"Mom, Dad and Trey are here with me."

"Morning, Sister." Distracted Miranda waved to a passing usher, who was busy looking from Caleb to Kelly. Miranda would bet that there would be rumors all over the church by the end of the choir worship that Kelly was their child.

"Chin up, sweetness. My mother's been dying to see you and meet Kelly."

His words, coupled with a friendly hand squeeze, instantly distracted her and she looked toward the front row. Sure enough, Caleb's mother, resplendent in an ivory-colored church hat, was smiling back at her.

She caught a sideways look as Caleb playfully began to swing Kelly's arm and her heart seemed to squeeze a little. Maybe it was the way he'd smiled at her when he'd greeted them earlier. It could have been because his eyes held a look of admiration, and his smile was filled with warmth. Maybe it was the way his hand felt in hers, or the pride she felt walking next to him.

All she knew was that some invisible ball of tension within her started to unravel.

His parents and brother stood up and hugged both her and Kelly.

Somehow Miranda came to be seated between Caleb and his mother. Knowing there was no escape, she aimed a frustrated glance in his direction. Their eyes locked and he winked before devoting his attention to Kelly. Miranda's teeth ground together.

"Miranda-dear, I am so glad you've forgiven Caleb."

Her attention snapped back to Mrs. Blackfox.

"I didn't really have a choice," she replied ruefully. "Your son is very persistent."

"All the men in this family are, I'm afraid. But I've known your mother and I've played a few hands of bridge with your aunt Patricia. I am sure you are more than able to keep Caleb in line."

"Now, sweetheart, don't go pressuring the dear girl," her husband interjected.

Mrs. Blackfox aimed a look at her husband—a look that gave Miranda a flashback. It was that one single glance that only a woman could make that would quiet any child. She gave him the type of look that promised severe and long-lasting repercussions.

Miranda stifled a laugh. Apparently it worked on grown men as well. Mr. Blackfox's mouth shut in a hurry and he turned the other way to talk with his son. She made a mental note to try it on Caleb when the next opportunity arose.

"Don't mind my husband. Now, are you and that little girl of yours going to be free this weekend?"

"We haven't planned anything. I'm just here to take care of my brother."

"Caleb told me about the car accident. I think it's a wonderful thing for you to come home and take care of him in your parents' absence. If you need anything, please let me know."

"Thank you. I think Kelly and I have it covered. We just have to keep him from doing something crazy like driving with a broken leg."

"Now back to my earlier question. We're having a little family get-together and a slumber party for the kids. I want you and Kelly to be there and I won't take no for an answer."

"Did you hear that, Miranda?"

She jumped when Caleb whispered in her ear. "My mother won't take no for an answer."

She blushed recalling all the times he'd managed to corner her in the house after examining her brother. Each time, he'd invited her out to dinner or over to his house and she'd politely declined even as he'd swooped down and kissed her senseless.

Feeling trapped between being polite and being stubborn, she chose to be polite and pasted a smile on her face. "We would love to come."

Miranda glanced at Caleb from the corner of her eyes and watched him aim a smirk in his brother's direction. Her eyes narrowed even further at Trey's thumbs-up signal. It didn't take a genius for her to figure out that she'd been set up. "I hate you," she whispered.

His lips twitched with a suppressed smile. "Remember, Hate is one of the seven deadly sins. I'm sure you don't mean that. Don't forget we're in the Lord's house."

"You're such a hypocrite."

"What do you mean?"

"Lust is on that 'seven deadly' list, isn't it?"

His eyes danced with mischief. "You must be mistaken. I believe in practicing the commandments. Right now I'm actively practicing Love Thy Neighbor."

But before she could voice her suspicions, the reverend stepped up to the podium and everyone stood for the opening benediction.

Irritated beyond belief, Miranda childishly reached out and pinched his arm. But before she could withdraw her hand he caught it and held it within his own. Aware of the looks they were getting from the choir, she ceased struggling to get her hand back.

"Good morning…good morning. The sun is shining and the birds are singing. For this brief time, you are in God's house and all is right with the world. I just want to start by saying we all know life ain't easy. Events and people in our lives will cause much joy and great sorrow."

Reverend Williams walked toward the front of the stage. "There are times when life just doesn't seem worth living. Mornings that you just don't want to get out of the bed. You just want to lie there and close your eyes. Could be that your kids have gone and done something stupid, your man done left you with bills unpaid, could be your job or maybe, just maybe, it's you. You just don't know what to do with your life, or with your family. Instead of thinking, you get angry. Why? 'Cause it's easy. It's easier to blame than accept, simpler to fear and hate than understand."

Placing his hands on either side of the podium, he leaned forward. "I want to tell you one fact. Nothing worth having comes cheap and the world doesn't owe you a dime. Let me tell you that life won't be fair, especially for those of African descent. But we have to get past that…we have to move on, move up and get over the mountain."

He raised his hands and pointed toward the congregation. Miranda felt as though he were pointing at their pew.

"I know it's hard, but today I am going to remind you about a gift that the Lord has bestowed upon his children. The gift is that of love, compassion and strength. The gift is one of faith and devotion. If there is something in your life weighing you down, give it to the Lord. Loneliness, sadness, doubt and anger setting up shop in your heart, give them to the Lord. All you have to do is ask and your wish will be granted, seek and you will find. I am going to close today not only with a prayer but also with a gift. I'm doing something different this morning. I'm going to make this sermon a short and powerful one."

Miranda looked toward one of the church deacons and had to bite her tongue to keep from giggling out loud. Deacon Jacob's eyes widened and he jerked back slightly. The Reverend Williams was well known for his two-and-a-half hour sermons.

The reverend took his place at the podium. "I know ya'll are shocked. Well, don't get used to it," he said smiling.

"When you depart this house of worship, I want the following prayer in your minds and in your hearts. Now close your eyes and repeat after me—

"God, grant me the serenity to accept the things I cannot change, the courage to change the things I can, and the wisdom to know the difference. Amen."

After the service Miranda somehow managed to get separated from Kelly and her family and Caleb's. Not only was it uncomfortable to be in the receiving end of all the knowing glances, it was downright irritating that Caleb wouldn't let go of her hand.

"Where are we going?" she asked as he led them out of the sanctuary.

"Here," he said.

Miranda's eyes widened as the exit door closed. *Here* turned out to be an empty stairwell leading to the upper balcony.

She blinked and found her back against the wall, looking up into Caleb's hungry stare. Scandalized and titillated at the same time, she forced back a hysterical giggle. "We're going to get struck by lightning, Caleb Blackfox."

"The Lord will approve since he knows we're just practicing."

Her tongue darted out to moisten her lips as her heart skipped a beat. "Practicing?"

His fingertips reached out and gently arched her chin upward.

"For when we say our *I do's*." The deep base of his voice reverberated across her skin.

She had time to draw a quick breath; then his mouth settled on hers, kissing her forcefully, almost punishing her mouth. His tongue pushed against her lips and forced its way into her mouth. Yet she kissed him back eagerly. Her closed hands opened and lay against his chest, her fingers clenching and unclenching against the lapels of his jacket as the dimly lit stairwell faded into a hazy oblivion. Miranda's eyes fluttered wide, and then shut. He held her there with one hand, cupped her hip and pulled her into even more intimate contact while his other hand traveled with achingly tender slowness up her spine to the nape of her neck.

This is not happening.

They were kissing in a stairwell in her family's church.

Only the sound of her own soft moan snapped her back to reality. She pulled back. When Miranda opened her eyes, she found Caleb grinning.

"So are you going to make an honest man of me?"

She stared at him. Though she knew he was joking, she couldn't really pay attention. Her pulse was racking, her ears were ringing. She was still suffering from the aftereffects of the kiss. Miranda inhaled deeply, forcing her mind to concentrate. Only it was useless. Maybe she was going crazy?

Caleb glanced down at the watch on his wrist and then back at her. "You have approximately five minutes to answer that question before my brother realizes where I'm hiding you."

The serious tone washed over her like a cool shower. She drew a breath when his questioning eyes came up to meet hers. She blinked and continued to just look at him. This was crazy, she told herself. It was impulsive and dangerous, and... exciting. Kissing in the church. What if they'd been caught? But there was something about Caleb that had always been irresistible; not to mention that he made her feel good. Real good. Like "the top of the world" good.

She swallowed. "I'm sorry, but did you just ask me to marry you?"

"Are you going to say yes?"

"I can't."

Caleb's shoulders relaxed. "I guess that beats a flat-out no. Remember the offer's still on the table. Now, how about we find Kelly and get you to your car?"

Gaping, Miranda allowed him to take her hand and lead her back into the main church building.

How could she have anticipated he would have pulled a stunt like that? Oh well, what did it matter? The sky was falling and she had fallen in love.

Chapter 14

Miranda and Kelly made it to her aunt and uncle's house just in time for Sunday dinner. The house was filled with the distinct aroma of Southern home cooking. She left her purse on the table in the entryway, and then hung her suit jacket in the closet.

"We're here," she yelled out.

"Miranda, why don't you come into the kitchen and have Kelly go downstairs and check on your uncle?"

"Is he okay?" Kelly asked as Miranda helped her take off her coat.

"Uncle Alan's fine. That was just my aunt's

way of saying that she wanted to talk to me alone."

Kelly's expression took on a sober tone and Miranda quickly tugged on a ponytail. "Don't worry. Uncle Alan has all kinds of neat stuff downstairs and I'm sure he could use your help on the computers."

"You uncle has a computer?" she asked suspiciously. Miranda had to giggle. Somehow the eleven-year-old had gotten it into her head that people over the age of thirty didn't know how to use the technology they created.

"I'll let you in on a secret. Uncle Alan can build computers."

Kelly's eyes grew to the size of silver pieces. "I wanna see!"

"Two seconds," Miranda said as she slipped out of her heels and left them in the hall closet. As stylish as her pumps were, she wished they'd been more comfortable. The moment she and Kelly stepped into the finished basement, the little girl's face lit up at the sight of the multiple computer screens and robotic toys.

Miranda observed for a few minutes before slipping back upstairs. It was past time she faced the music, and knowing her aunt she'd be ready to sing.

"It smells great in here, Auntie Pat," Miranda said as she crossed the kitchen to the sink and washed her hands.

"You could have at least sent a wedding invitation. You could have said something to prepare us for your coming home with an eleven-year-old child in tow. Do your parents even know what you've been up to? That would be impossible. Your mother can't keep a secret, so you must not have told her."

"I don't want them worrying about me." Miranda dried her hands.

"Well, someone needs to." A smile played at the corner of her mouth. "Maybe this is just what needs to happen in this family to get Margaret and David to come home. I pray for them every night and I send money to those orphaned kids every month."

As crazy as the cover story was, the surprising thing was that everyone had believed her. Most likely because no one could fathom that Miranda Tyler could ever tell a lie. Her stomach twisted and she wondered why she didn't have nightmares. Even after the stunt Caleb had pulled at church, she wanted him. He made her feel again, to need again, to want things that she'd promised herself she could never risk again. Love. Commitment. Marriage. When he'd kissed her in the stairwell with the choir singing in the background, it was as if the Lord had blessed her. When Caleb held her, she forgot about the past and allowed herself to hope. With him she risked losing her heart again.

This is why I need to stay away from him.

Miranda sighed inwardly as she reached into the cabinet and pulled down a glass. He was going to make it impossible. Before she left Georgia, they would know each other in a very Biblical sense. She knew that like she knew her own name. When they were close, her body reacted. Hidden underneath her bra, her nipples were hard and sensitive. Her pulse beat erratically and her stomach warmed. Even her mouth longed to taste his skin. The question was, how would she handle what happens next?

Since she'd seen her aunt after the sermon, the woman had changed out of her church clothes and was busy moving around the kitchen in her gourmet apron. Miranda hid a smile behind her glass of sweet tea as her mother's best friend and older sister fussed around the kitchen. Any moment now the scent of roasted chicken, mushrooms, and macaroni and cheese would come wafting from the oven.

With all the change that had occurred in the past few weeks, going to church that morning and then stopping by her aunt's house had been just what she'd needed to regain a little balance. Walking through the home and looking at portraits of her great-grandparents, grandparents, cousins, aunts and uncles strengthened her sense of family.

"Miranda, you've gotten too thin. What have you been eating?" Aunt Pat's dark eyes scanned her frame while Miranda opened the refrigerator to pull out a carafe of sweet tea. "I know you haven't been eating right. You need to get some more meat on your bones."

Aunt Pat lightly pinched Miranda's arm. "I don't want to hear no mess about either of you picking up that supermodel disease. I won't have any…"

"Anorexia," Miranda supplied after pouring more tea and returning it to the refrigerator.

Aunt Pat nodded her head. Patricia Russell looked fantastic. She walked two miles a day and her auburn-colored hair was pulled back in a stylish French twist.

"That's the one," she declared. "We won't have it in this family."

"Auntie," Miranda protested with a smile on her face as she sat down at the kitchen counter. "I'm in no danger of becoming anorexic."

The women in her family were big-boned. No matter how much time Miranda spent on the Stairmaster at the gym, her backside wasn't going anywhere. It was a gift from someone on her mother's side of the family with a no-money-back, no-return, no-exchange policy attached.

"Don't *auntie* me. I'm still upset about your little marriage misadventure."

"I know," she replied and prayed that her aunt wouldn't ask too many questions. Miranda hated lying, especially to family, but ever since she volunteered to keep Kelly hidden she'd been doing a lot of it. And the scary part was that she was getting better at not telling the truth. All throughout the church service, Miranda had been praying that God wouldn't strike her down for the falsehoods she'd had to tell the people.

Only looking down at Kelly's bright eyes and knowing the real danger her father was in kept Miranda going. She couldn't imagine having to do it for the rest of her life. And for the first time she really understood what people gave up to be in the Witness Protection Agency. She already felt as if she'd given up her conscience.

"You know I'm going to be dodging phone calls from all of the deacons' wives tonight. Not only did you come home with a child in tow, but you've managed to grab the attention of Dr. Caleb Blackfox. You would think that he'd be a little less obvious in his courting technique. Not to mention that family of his. I know that the Blackfox family is close, but did he need to bring the entire clan to the service? The church secretary almost fainted when he looked down at the collection plate."

"I had no idea that Caleb would be in church this morning."

"I could tell that. So what really happened? Why did you get a divorce?"

"Simple. Ryan and I were good friends, not good mates."

"Well he should have done things the old-fashioned way and talked to your father first. I know he would have set both of you straight."

"He'd wanted to but I convinced him not to. I didn't want to come home yet."

"Still mourning Caleb, weren't you?"

"Yes," she said simply.

"And your stubborn rear end jumped in front of a bus."

"Something like that. But I didn't get hit. Ryan's wife had died and I needed help taking care of Kelly. It wasn't all that bad."

"I still think you're holding out. To be married to a man for a few years and not even tell your parents? And you must have taken off your rings because I would not have been able to miss seeing a wedding band."

"I did."

"And where was Ms. Kelly when you came home?"

"She spent time with Ryan's family. Both her mother and father were only children so we are the only family she has."

"You best remember that. That little girl is family. Your uncle is down in the basement right now showing off his computer network."

"And I'm sure she's loving every second of it."

"Just like you were when Dr. Blackfox made a show of sitting beside you in church."

"Can we change the subject?"

"Why? Are you uncomfortable, niece of mine?"

Miranda was about to roll her eyes until she remembered who she was talking to. The childhood memories, including threats of being slapped back to slavery, held her eyes straight ahead. "Very," she added dryly.

"Then you're going to squirm in your chair when I tell you that I caught your doctor giving me the eye."

Miranda was so startled she choked on her iced tea. After coughing up a storm and wiping tears from her eyes she rasped, "What?"

"Yep. His father, too. If you ask me they were just looking at me to figure out how you're going to look in twenty years. Don't let that mess fool you. Your uncle had been checking out your grandmother before he even looked at me."

"And how do you know that, Auntie?"

"You know your uncle Alan thinks he's the smartest man in the county. Take him to a party and I can guarantee that on the second glass of

Hennessy, he'll start bragging about how he has the prettiest woman in Georgia and all that."

Miranda laughed at the lovingly sarcastic tone in her aunt's voice. "Well, both you and Mom were homecoming queens."

Aunt Pat smiled and waved a hand. "That was then, this is now. You've finally come back home. I just wish you'd stop being so tight-lipped about that Blackfox son."

"What do you want to know?"

"Are you in love with him?" she asked bluntly.

Miranda winced, sat back in the chair and swallowed hard. Was she in love with Caleb? She didn't really have anything to compare her emotions to. With Ryan they'd dated, kissed, held hands, talked for hours. But she couldn't even fool herself when it came to love because she'd experienced it before. Her heart knew what real love felt like. She'd been in love with Caleb Blackfox. Her mind rushed through a list of semi-believable responses to her aunt's question and she settled on one. "I will probably always care for Caleb. He was my first love."

"That wasn't what I asked. Remember you stayed at my house for a few days that summer after you graduated from college. I've got first-hand knowledge of the shape you were in after breaking up with him. Not to mention your mother called me every night and all we did was talk about you. Now, my daughter just went through some mess with her last boyfriend and that nonsense gave your uncle and me a few gray hairs."

"I'm not sure, Auntie. I'm taking this one slow."

"I'm hoping that's because you learned your lesson with your last relationship."

Miranda sighed again. "Of course."

"Momma, I just looked at the top of our house from a satellite. It's so cool. Your uncle is so cool."

Miranda smiled as she watched Kelly jump into the seat next to hers. She turned her cheek and caught her uncle Alan's grin.

"Kelly, why don't you wash your hands and help me put the frosting on this red velvet cake I baked last night? If you do a good job, I'll let you lick the bowl."

Just like that her aunt's focus shifted to the little girl. Miranda sat back alongside her uncle.

Cooking was Aunt Pat's pride and joy; the kitchen her domain. The men in the family were only allowed to watch her work and to later pay proper praise to her delicious meals, while the youngest girls were drafted as visiting apprentices.

"She sure does know how to handle your little girl." Her uncle had leaned in close to whisper in Miranda's ear.

"Maybe we should take lessons?" she whispered.

"Don't know about you, but I've been taking notes for some time. How you think I kept her from leaving me?" Uncle Alan replied.

"By eating?" she joked.

They burst into laughter. When Miranda looked up with tears in her eyes, Aunt Pat and Kelly had the two of them in their sights.

Miranda watched her aunt raise her eyebrow. "Anything the two of you'd like to share?" she asked.

"Nah." She shook her head quickly.

"Are you sure?" Aunt Pat looked from her husband's smiling face back to Miranda's.

"Uh-huh."

"Positive," Uncle Alan answered, giving her hand a little squeeze.

"I'm going to make a plate for that brother of yours. I'm sure he isn't eating right. And you'd better tell him that he needs to be in church next week."

Miranda sat back and let out a breath when Kelly asked Aunt Pat a question and the woman's laser-sharp eyes returned to cooking. Miranda was safe for a moment, but her thoughts drifted back to Caleb. During and after the service that devastating grin of his was in full effect. Without a doubt, the uptilt of his generous lips and perfect white teeth would appear in her fantasies. What was it about Caleb that made her want to throw caution into the winds and forget about the lies she'd told, the bad breakup, and concentrate on satisfying her curiosity as to what he looked like naked in bed?

Swallowing a sigh, she stared down at the white napkin. Maybe it was time she threw in the towel and surrendered? Maybe if she spent the night with Caleb, it would get him out of her system. Yep, just took him to bed and kept him there all night. A secret smile tugged her lips upward. Dr. Blackfox was about to get exactly what he wanted and he didn't even know it.

Later on that night, after getting home from church, Miranda warmed up Darren's plate in the microwave and grudgingly delivered the meal to his room. With Kelly in her room happily occupied with a Sodoku book, Miranda began to tackle the chores.

First she finished the laundry, and then vacuumed the living room, dining room, then the den. Still awake and preoccupied with keeping her thoughts off the upcoming week of seeing Caleb every day, she opened the dishwasher and began to put away the dishes.

"Kelly told me to tell you good-night." Darren's voice startled her and she looked up to see him struggling to put the plate on the open bar. When he'd successfully landed the plate, Darren had managed to drop his crutches and maneuver himself onto the bar stool.

"Why didn't she come in to tell me herself?"

"She was afraid you might make her clean," he stated matter-of-factly.

Miranda aimed a quizzical glance his way. "Why on earth would she think something like that? She has school tomorrow."

"I was scared to come in myself. What kind of woman vacuums at eight o'clock at night?"

"A clean one," she replied tartly.

"Whatever. I heard about the show you and Caleb put on at the church this morning."

"Did Aunt Pat call you?"

"No. I got a call from one of my buddies."

"Look, Darren." Miranda cut in quickly, not wanting to hear again the list of Caleb's limitless sins. "I know what you're going to say."

"No, you don't."

"Really?" She aimed a skeptical glance his way, and then returned to the task of putting up the plates.

"Yes. I'm here to tell you that it was my fault."

"*Your* fault?" she repeated. "What are you talking about?"

"I was the one who broke up you and Blackfox all those years ago."

Miranda froze with shock and then unfroze. She turned, crossed her arms over her chest and stared at her brother. "Go on."

He looked down at his fingers. "I had a good friend at Morehouse. You probably never met the guy. I drove down over spring break and we went to a few parties, had some drinks. I mentioned that I didn't like the boy my sister was dating and I wanted to break them up. It just happened that he had a cousin at Spellman who had her eye on Blackfox."

"Let me guess, Jessica Greene wasn't it?" Miranda said flatly.

"Yeah."

Her emotions at that moment ran the gauntlet from disbelief to anger, and finally settled on resignation. "Why, Darren?"

"I never thought I'd hurt you the way I did. Or that you'd leave the state."

"No." She shook her head. "I meant why are you telling me now?"

"Because I was wrong. Because I can't deny the fact that Blackfox loves you. And as much as I hate to admit it, he makes you happy," he grumbled.

"Repeat that first part. I didn't hear you."

"I was wrong, damn it. If someone were to do something to try and break up Grace and me, I would…"

"Kill them," Miranda supplied.

Darren swallowed and looked guilty. "That's a little dramatic, don't you think?"

"Maybe…maybe not," Miranda threatened, even though she didn't mean it. She couldn't put a hundred percent of the blame on her brother's shoulders. The seeds of insecurity and distrust had been planted in their relationship long before that night. Not to mention that neither Miranda nor Caleb had been ready for a serious relationship. But now? She shook her head. Not as long as she couldn't come clean about her bogus ex-husband and adopted daughter.

"Come on, Randa," her brother pleaded. "Say something. It's not like I did it to deliberately hurt you."

"But you did hurt me."

"I'm apologizing. It's a 'fifteen years and I wish I could do it all over again and I would do it differently' kind of apology. Please don't leave me hanging, because I really need some forgiveness."

She didn't say a word for a moment longer, enjoying watching him squirm. She walked over and, careful of his braced arm, delicately hugged him.

"Does that mean you're forgiving me?"

She pulled back and smiled softly. "Of course, knucklehead."

Darren let out a loud breath of sheer relief. "That was easy."

"I just hope it's that easy when I tell Caleb the truth."

"It will be," he said simply.

Miranda chewed on her lips and released a sigh.

If only she had his confidence.

Chapter 15

She'd finally given in and agreed to come to Caleb's house to discuss the search for his great-uncle only to be left standing alone in the man's foyer.

Miranda smiled ruefully—the minute he'd opened the door for her the hospital had called. It was great that she had a healthy dose of self-confidence or she'd be jealous of his work.

Although she'd dated numerous men in Washington, D.C., Miranda had never ventured into their homes and had assumed that they'd be Spartan bachelor pads. But what she found walking through the door to Caleb's house had momentarily taken her breath away. Beyond the entranceway, the foyer stretched for yards in front of her, continuing into a high-ceiling anteroom. Open arched doorways lined each side, and the end of the hallway was a large window filled with the light of the setting sun. The house was just as she might have imagined it would be: fit for a doctor and beautifully designed and decorated.

With her coat still buttoned, Miranda walked forward, her loafers whispering over the marble before stepping onto hardwood floors. To her right, a mahogany wrought-iron staircase curved upward to the second floor. She reached out and trailed a hand over the banister leading up the stairs. Even to her untrained eye, she could see that it was the product of a master craftsman.

Even the air was nicely perfumed with hints of vanilla and sandalwood. She turned to the right and paused in astonishment. The living room, or at least what she assumed was a living room, had exquisitely designed furniture and decorative accents, a large stone-encased fireplace and plush rugs. Miranda kept going and passed through the dining room, gourmet kitchen, and stopped in the last room. Her hand came up to cover her mouth as she laughed. The room was Darren's dream come to life. Leather sofas faced a wall-spanning flat-screen television surrounded by every audio, video and gaming device money could buy. A bar occupied another section of the room and a billiard table stood opposite.

"Like what you see?"

Miranda jumped at the sound of Caleb's voice. "Good Lord, I think you took five years off my life."

"I didn't mean to startle you."

Shaking her head, Miranda let out a small giggle. "It's not your fault you move as silently as a ghost."

"Yep, it's my brother's fault. Marius taught us how to walk quietly so that we could sneak past my parents' room."

"Why doesn't it surprise me that you snuck out when you were a teenager?"

"Oh, we were sneaking out of the house way before we were teenagers. There was this clear meadow about a mile away from the house. Whenever there was a full moon, we'd sneak out to the barn, saddle the horses and race against some of the neighbors."

"You're kidding?"

"Scout's honor. I won more than I lost—but I lost a lot."

"Because your horse was slow?"

He grimaced. "No. My sister either beat me, or the horse crossed the finish line without me. I wasn't much of a rider."

"But you did it anyway." She smiled.

"There's nothing like the invincibility of youth. Now can I take your coat?"

His fingertips glanced over the nape of her neck and Miranda barely suppressed an answering shiver as she removed the long coat.

"You have a beautiful home."

"Thank you, but," Caleb gently corrected her, "I have a house. Your parents, my parents and my family have homes."

She followed him into the kitchen and stopped next to the granite-topped island. The room was far from homey. She could have honestly been standing in a Williams-Sonoma print ad. Gray commercial-size anodized pots and pans hung from strategically placed hooks over the stove, and sleek gourmet culinary accessories sat neatly on the countertops, while high-end appliances nestled underneath. "It wouldn't take much to make this into a home, Caleb. I think all you have to do is to spend more time here than at the hospital."

"My mother and Aunt Lacey tried to make sure that this place had everything I needed. But the point is that I'm not needed here. I'm needed at the hospital."

"But what if you were needed here, Caleb?" she asked softly.

"Then this is where I would be." Caleb removed two wineglasses and gently set them down before continuing. "With my wife, with my family."

Miranda's body was so taut with emotion that she could hardly speak. Just the thought of Caleb with some unknown woman felt like someone had taken a knife to her insides. Ever since they'd reunited at the hospital, her feelings had gotten the best of her even as her better judgment screamed at her not to trust him. Not to trust the sincerity in his voice, the sweet promise of happiness in his eyes. He'd been honest before, but had still ended up breaking her heart. Yet, no matter how many times she whispered to herself that what was between them couldn't last because she had her job in Washington, the fact didn't stop her heart from wanting him or her fingers from itching to touch him and unbutton his shirt.

Recalling the other reason she was at his home, Miranda managed, "Would you like to review the detective's notes on your uncle's case?"

"Of course. Just thought I'd pour a glass of wine and prepare cheese and crackers. Unless you object to having some small comfort while we work?"

"No, not at all."

"Good. I'll get the snacks together. Why don't you choose the wine. I have white, Zinfandel, Shiraz, you name it."

"Why would I be the least surprised that this dream would come equipped with a wine cellar?"

"It's not really a cellar." Caleb grinned as he took both of their glasses and started walking in the direction of the library. "More like a converted closet."

"Isn't it the man's job to pick out the wine?"

"If I recall correctly, you, madame, dragged me to a few wine-tastings after your twenty-first birthday."

She smiled and nibbled on her bottom lip. "So I did. Where can I find this collection of yours?"

"Straight through to the entertainment room and it's the second door on your left."

"Can you at least give me some selection criteria? It's been years since I've had anything to do with wine outside of an occasional glass at a restaurant."

"Red."

Okay, Miranda mused, this ought to be easy. That was until she opened the door and walked into a temperature-controlled wall-to-wall bottle-filled wine closet.

"You have got to be kidding," she shouted.

"You can do it."

"Good Lord, Caleb," she muttered as her eyes took in the rows of bottles. "This is too much. No one needs this much wine."

"It's not for quantity. It's for selection," he said.

She jumped and turned, hearing his voice so close to her ear. Letting out a shaky breath, Miranda playfully punched him on the shoulder. "You just took another year off my life. Could you make some more noise next time?"

"I'll try."

"I can't pick a wine, Caleb."

"When was it? I remember—the night we went out to dinner to officially celebrate the anniversary of our first date."

"You took me to that wonderful Italian restaurant."

"Soto's," he added. "I try to go there when I get down to Atlanta."

"I loved the ravioli." Miranda's mouth watered at the mere memory.

"The chefs may have changed, but the owners haven't. And remember what he said when I needed to select a wine?"

Miranda's brow wrinkled as she tried to retrieve the memory. Yet all she could think about was the wonder of that night. The fantastic meal, the romantic candlelit dancing in Caleb's apartment, and making love on a bed of rose petals.

"No."

"Well, I do. And he said, 'Light foods go with light wines. Heavy foods go with heavy wines. Delicate meals need a light wine. Heavier meals need a bigger wine.'"

Miranda nodded. "And where does cheese and crackers fit into that?"

"I also forgot to mention that we're having cheesecake bites."

Miranda groaned. "My waistline, doctor. I didn't come home to gain thirty pounds on vacation."

"You can use every pound, Miranda."

"Let's not get distracted. Pick a wine."

Caleb shook his head and laughed. The sound filled the intimate space and turned her insides to jelly.

"No, beautiful. This is your assignment."

If possible, he seemed to stand even closer to her. Miranda stood with her back to Caleb and she could feel the warm trickle of his breath on the back of her bare neck. And she so badly wanted his strong arms to wrap around her waist, so she could lean back and indulge in wonderful feelings of contentment.

"You've got to give me a hint at least, Caleb."

He blew out a choked breath that sounded suspiciously like laughter. "Close your eyes and choose one."

"Why can't you do this? You're the one with the collection," she stressed, giving him an irritated glare.

He leaned in closer. "I've a secret."

"What?"

"I didn't buy any of this, someone else did."

Her eyes widened. "So you don't know what to get, either..."

"You're wounding my pride right now. All of my brothers think that I'm a wine expert."

"I won't tell a soul." Spying what she thought was a nicely decorated bottle, Miranda took a step toward the back wall housing a selection of red wines, and pulled out what she hoped was a good bottle.

"Pinot Noir, 1988. This has to be a good year," she proclaimed.

"Why's that?" Caleb asked as they returned to the kitchen.

"That was the year I got straight A's on my report card and Darren and I got our braces taken off."

"You had braces?"

"All of us aren't born blessed with perfect teeth."

"I had to wear a retainer for three years," he replied offhandedly.

Miranda's defensiveness vanished as she stared at Caleb. He never ceased to amaze her. He smiled and picked up a serving plate and walked through the open doorway that led to the den. The square hardwood table in the corner was set for two. The curtains had been drawn back to reveal a clear winter-night sky. She took a seat across from him and settled herself in the nice-size wooden chair. He expertly popped the cork. Miranda's eyes never left his as he filled two glasses with deep red wine.

When he handed her a goblet, their fingers

touched, and her breath caught in her chest. There was a moment of staring too long, a jolt, a shiver. She shook her head to clear herself of the dangerous thoughts.

"Cheers," he said and raised his glass. Clicking his glass with hers, Caleb noted the way the lights picked up the highlights in Miranda's thick mane. He'd always been fascinated by her hair. And on more than one occasion he'd enjoyed making her moan with pleasure just by massaging sensitive locations on her scalp.

"Here's to successful careers, safe loved ones, smooth recoveries and to finding your great-uncle," Miranda responded and took a sip. Her face relaxed, eyes closed, as she smelled and then tasted the smooth pinot noir.

Caleb pictured that look of repletion as she lay beneath him in his bed. Her dilated eyes heavy with lovemaking, her skin flushed and her moans of pleasure arousing.

Just thinking about her had his body tight with anticipation. Maybe he should run upstairs and take a shower and let the cold water calm him down. No. That brought a flashback of the times that they'd showered together at his condo before going to class. He blinked slowly at the image of Miranda peeling off her robe and stepping into the steam-filled bathroom.

Making no effort to savor the wine, Caleb lifted

his glass and took a large mouthful in one swallow. "Funny you should toast to successful careers. I've been thinking a lot about the future now that I've been at the hospital for a few years."

"Any ideas?"

"Private practice, academics or a physician's group. Mom is pushing for me to join with her church-affiliated medical practice."

"That might not be such a bad thing."

"It is when you're not married," he replied after taking a bite of cheese.

"You could specialize in male ailments," she suggested.

"I don't think that ruse would work any better." He shook his head. "Besides having every single churchgoing female on the patient list, it would be impossible keeping my mother out of my personal life. I'm having a hard time of it now."

"Oh, well." She sighed. "Looks like the nurses at the hospital will be able to sleep better knowing that their eye candy won't be stolen."

"Eye candy? So you think I'm sweet." The intent look in his eyes and low voice was drop-dead sexy.

Miranda took a sip of wine and smiled. Tomorrow morning, when she remembered the evening, she'd blame her behavior on the alcohol. Or maybe she would blame Caleb. The only thing Miranda knew for certain was that it was fun to flirt and the way he kept looking at her had started a miniheat wave in the valley in her thighs. "Oh, sorry. I meant to say that their easy-going doctor won't be stolen."

"That's worse not better. I'd rather be eye candy. I've always thought of myself as straw-berry rock candy like the homemade kind I pur-chased during our trip to Gatlinburg."

She shook her head. "No, too hard, too sweet and way too crunchy. You're a chocolate bar. Rich, deep and loaded with calories."

"Dark chocolate?" He laughed heartily. "I seem to remember that you at one time were addicted to the stuff."

"I went into Chocolate Addicts Anonymous after my twenty-sixth birthday," she replied with a straight face while giggles bubbled in her throat.

Caleb nibbled on a piece of cheese, fully re-laxed in the leather chair. He couldn't know how utterly handsome he looked like that—his brow puckered with a frown, biceps stretching the long sleeves of his turtleneck sweater.

His eyes darkened, almost midnight. "I think I have some chocolate chip cookies and candy bars stashed away somewhere. All you have to do is say the word."

Miranda burst out laughing because that was all she could do. Somewhere deep inside her, a rational person was screaming that the Miranda Tyler she knew would never ever consider getting back together with the man who'd broken her heart. She was completely over him and looking forward to meeting the man of her dreams.

Yet somehow the rational Miranda got drowned out by the somewhat uninhibited and impulsive Miranda, who wondered what color boxers Caleb wore underneath his slacks—blue, green or white?

"Miranda?"

The sound of her name interrupted her illicit thoughts.

"I'm sorry." Miranda blushed as she met his concerned stare. "What did you say?"

"How about a quick game of checkers before we get to work?" he asked.

She shook her head. "I'm not sure."

"Afraid to lose?"

"No," she bit back. "I'm just not used to leaving Kelly alone for so long."

"She's not alone."

"True, she's with my recuperating brother. There's no telling what kinds of trouble those two could get into."

Seeming to ignore her response, Caleb reached over, opened a door on the built-in shelving unit and pulled out a leather-encased box.

"First, Kelly and Darren are probably sitting in front of the television playing video games, eating popcorn and drinking soda. Second, they have your cell phone number if they need you. Third,

I think that you're trying to use them as an excuse because you've forgotten how to play."

"Forgotten how to play?" She tried to bluff and then looked into Caleb's amused face. "To be honest, I haven't played checkers in years."

"Then I promise to take it easy on you." He laughed.

"This set looks pretty expensive," Miranda observed. Reaching out she ran a finger over the white and red pieces. Instead of the usual plastic, she encountered smooth stone.

Once Caleb finished setting up the board, he responded, "It's one of a dozen like it. My grandfather had them made for all the grandkids one Christmas. You first."

She took a sip of wine before placing her finger on the black checker to make the first advance.

"So I take it you're really into checkers?" she asked.

"Dad loves checkers. Some fathers taught their children sports. He taught us all how to drive a truck, ride a horse, shoot a gun, play checkers and poker. My uncles taught us how to play a mean hand of Texas hold 'em."

"Texas hold 'em?" she asked.

"Poker. It's a family tradition that one Saturday a month, the menfolk get together, play cards and drink until they pass out," Caleb said after taking a jump.

Miranda couldn't resist the opportunity to jump one of his checkers on her next move.

"Yes." He sighed. "After my first fight at school, Dad brought me into his study, sat me down and we played checkers until I'd lost all my allowance for the summer. He taught me that the mind is more powerful than the fist."

"We were all about playing cards in my family," Miranda responded while her eyes never left the board. "My mom can play a game of spades like nobody's business. Pop, my dad, taught us all how to play poker."

"Your dad taught you, too?"

She nodded and grimaced as he took advantage of a double jump and took two of her checkers. It was looking more and more like this wasn't going to be Miranda's night to win. "Every Saturday, my pop and his friends got together at our house to play cards in the basement. After the games were over, Pop would let Darren and I sit down at the table and play. We used jelly beans as a substitute for chips."

"So you're a card shark? I'll have to remember that." Caleb smiled as he moved his piece onto the last row. "Crown me."

"Sneak," she accused while placing a red checker over his.

"The woman is a sore loser." Caleb rubbed his chin.

Miranda shook her head. "The game isn't over yet."

"Spoken like a true fighter."

"That's right." She nodded. Placing her hand over her mouth she faked a yawn. "How about you give me the extra notes and I'll read them tomorrow? I'll have plenty of time during the day since I have to wake up early in the morning and make sure Kelly gets off to school."

"Really? She told me that she didn't have to go to school tomorrow—teachers' holiday. Besides, it's only eight o'clock."

She searched her memory and the answer almost made her lose a short curse word. Caleb was right. She'd forgotten that tomorrow was an in-school teacher training day.

"You're right, but it's good to keep the house on a schedule and I wake the earliest," she babbled. "You know the saying—early to bed."

Caleb didn't look the least bit happy as she stood up and stretched. "Guess you'll have to wait until next time before I beat you," she boasted.

"Sweetheart, you're losing."

Miranda cocked her head. "It's all about point of view. I'm not losing. I'm just about to make a comeback."

"God, you make it hard to think when you look at me like that, Miranda."

Caleb couldn't help himself as he moved to

stand in front of her. He reached up and drew his thumb along her jaw, tilting her chin to him. Just one quick taste, that's all he wanted and then he'd be able to concentrate. He leaned close and brushed his lips against hers, tracing her lips with the tip of his tongue. Mistake. The knowledge that he would never get enough of the woman in his arms penetrated his mind. His mouth hungered for the heady taste of her, and he needed her more with an urgency that grew each passing moment.

Miranda swayed forward to meet his kiss. Their lips and tongues played, and he tasted the red wine she'd just sipped. She was intoxicating, like wine, filling his mouth with lushness. How long they kissed, he couldn't tell and when Caleb finally regained the willpower to end it, he still couldn't let her go. Placing a kiss on her forehead, he hugged her close. "You don't want to trust me. You don't want to care for me. Hell, you probably don't even want to like me," he whispered. "But I feel as if we've been given a second chance. And I don't know about you but I won't let this slip away." He rested his forehead on her hair, breathing in the sweet scent of her.

Miranda didn't know what to think or what to say. He was right. She didn't want to feel anything for Caleb, but she did. The only things that was keeping her from throwing caution to the winds and giving in to the intense emotions coursing through her veins were memories. She still had memories of lying on the carpet of her parents' house because she couldn't breathe. The panic attacks of a broken heart, and the pain of loving someone that she couldn't have.

"Look, Caleb…" she started.

He held a finger against her lips. "I know that this is too much, too soon. I need to re-earn your love and your trust. I should not expect you to let go of the past. I should expect nothing. Just don't take away my hope."

Miranda inhaled sharply and the musky fragrance of his cologne sent another wave of passion throughout her slender frame. She looked away to hide the realization that she knew would show in her eyes; that after eleven years she was still in love with him. "Either you are the best con-artist who ever lived, Caleb Blackfox," she said, "or the luckiest man I've ever met." She reached up and placed her fingertips on either side of his face. "Either way, I want to make love, Caleb."

"Tell me I'm not dreaming, Miranda."

"You're not dreaming."

The combination of the words she spoke and her body language were music to his ears. For years after they'd broken up he'd still dreamed of them making love, and now she was there in his house, in his arms, telling him what he longed to hear.

He didn't respond to her statement verbally, but physically. He took her by the hand and led her upstairs to his bedroom. Letting go of her hand, he kicked off his shoes and watched as she looked around admiring the décor. It was a man's bedroom with its dark wood and heavy furniture. "Does the design meet your approval?" he asked.

Her dark eyes focused on him. "You meet my approval."

The spark of memories combined with the heady intoxication of their earlier kisses and Caleb forgot all about getting out of his clothes. It was far more important to get rid of hers. He took three steps forward and pulled Miranda into his arms. The instant their mouths touched, a passion born long ago exploded. He kissed her with everything he possessed and when her arms wrapped around his neck, Caleb felt like he was home.

Then, after regaining a measure of control, Caleb ended the kiss and gently touched his mouth to hers once, then twice. His eyes locked with hers.

"Are you sure?" he whispered, leaning closer to her lips. "Once I get you in that bed, Miranda, I'm not letting you out."

"Good, because all I want is for you to be in," she managed to respond. She placed a finger to his lips to convey the seriousness of what she was about to say. "What happens between us tonight happens between two very consenting adults. From the first moment I saw you at the hospital, I knew it would come to this."

That was all he needed to hear. Caleb had done some difficult things in his lifetime, but at the moment nothing compared to how hard it was not to rip off her clothes. She must have read his thoughts because she began to remove her sweater and pants. Wordlessly, he followed suit until there was nothing between them but bare skin.

Her breasts were high, round, the nipples pebbled to hardness.

A ragged sigh escaped him. "Do you know what you do to me?"

Miranda's head was tilted back, her eyes half-lidded as she looked up at him, and he could see her losing it a little. "No… Show me," she said softly.

Her words were his undoing. In an instant, he pulled her into his arms and kissed her over and over again. Like a starving man, he showered her neck, lips and her shoulders with kisses. Then he calmed down, exploring her body leisurely as he laid her down on the bed.

He moved his hand and gently cupped her breast, pulling his head away from her long enough to look up and catch her gaze…then he slowly guided the cocoa-tinted nipple into his mouth. Miranda hissed in her breath lightly. Caleb's other hand cupped her behind, squeezing the round flesh…then he pulled her closer, so close she had to put one hand on his shoulder to steady herself against his chest. He sucked her nipple gently, his eyes still holding hers, and then he gripped it lightly between his teeth, teasing the tip with a series of butterfly-light flutters of his tongue.

"Caleb," Miranda groaned at the featherlight kisses against her sensitive skin. Her breathing became unsteady and her muscles weakened as his hands paid tribute to her body. She moaned out loud and his fingers seemed to be everywhere. Unable to take any more, she gripped his head and pulled him upward for a kiss. "Come inside," she whispered against his mouth.

Caleb could barely breathe at her whispered command. When they were dating she'd leave him a note in his textbook with that phrase, and he'd barely make it through the day knowing that when he got home she'd be in his bed, naked. He didn't think it would have been possible to want her more, but somehow she'd managed to make that happen.

"Still a bossy little thing, aren't you?" he growled. Caleb took the delicate nub of her ear between his teeth and nibbled.

"Now…please…"

Caleb reached over to the nightstand, opened the drawer and pulled out a foil-lined packet. As he unwrapped one, Miranda levered herself up on her elbow and delicately began to nibble on his neck.

His hips instinctively jerked forward, and his hand hit against the headboard in an effort to keep his balance. "Woman, don't do that. I'm on edge."

Her brown eyes seemed to glow with sensual mischief. She took the condom from his fingers. It took every ounce of self-control he possessed to remain still while she slowly rolled it down the hardness of his manhood. Task accomplished, she explored him, cupped him with her soft, slender fingers. But he quickly took possession of her wrists with one of his hands and the other stroked her neck and breasts, while his lips took her mouth. Miranda opened her legs and felt him shift, fitting perfectly in place with her body.

"Open your eyes," he commanded.

She obeyed and their gazes locked. His fingers gripped her hips, holding her still as he entered her, withdrew, returned, and the sensation of emptiness gave way to the fullness of completion. He was warm and hard inside her. Miranda arched her hips taking him deeper inside, wanting him. The feel of his thrusting, coupled with his kisses pushed her closer to the edge as they found their rhythm. The last thing she felt was Caleb's hand stroking that sensitive spot before pleasure washed over her like a hard rain.

Miranda felt rather than heard Caleb's release as her body went tight. When he went limp and laid his head against her chest, she closed her eyes and gave in to the bone-melting postclimax relaxation. A dreamy smile curved her lips, and then disappeared. Something this wonderful couldn't last. She just hoped to keep it as long as possible.

In the early morning hours, before sunrise, Caleb, still half asleep, groaned as his alarm clock went off. Rolling over, his hand automatically reached out and hit the snooze button. His thoughts immediately retuned to the night before. Years of longing and passion had come to the forefront and they'd made love at least three times. He turned and reached across the sheets. The bed was empty. Caleb opened his eyes and fruitlessly scanned the bedroom. Although her scent lingered on his sheets, Miranda was long gone.

Chapter 16

The week sped by in a blur after leaving Caleb's place in the middle of the night, and then sneaking into her parents' house. Chasing new leads on Lucas Blackfox, PTA meetings and delivering documents for her brother took up most of her time. By Friday, Miranda would have happily curled up in her bed and slept. Instead, after helping Kelly pack her overnight bag for the sleepover with Caleb's family, she rushed into the bathroom. There wasn't much time left before the man himself arrived to take them to the party.

She quickly showered, then dried off and moisturized her body with vanilla-scented lotion. She added a spritz of perfume to her wrists and dabbed a little behind her ears, and then moved on to her hair. She'd had it professionally relaxed and trimmed a few weeks ago. Removing the pens that held her hair in a bun, she picked up her brush and ran it across her auburn black hair, smoothing down the sides. Her thick, below-the-ear hair held a hint of honey highlights she'd gotten the past summer. A satisfied smile crinkled the corners of her mouth as she examined the result in the mirror. Not wanting to waste any more of the time that she didn't have, she reached for her makeup case, dabbed on a little mascara, and a light stain of lipstick. Miranda lightly applied a little blush to her cheekbones, and then slipped into her dress and a pair of mules.

She had just run back to her room and was in the process of putting on her earrings when the doorbell rang. Her heart flipped over.

"I'll get it," Kelly shouted before hurrying out of her room and into the hallway.

"No, you won't," Miranda countered. "Remember what I told you about that."

"But I know it's Dr. Caleb."

"And how can you be so sure?"

Kelly rolled her eyes. "I looked through the window."

"Fine, brat. Why don't you finish checking to see if you have everything while I get the door?"

"Okay."

Miranda paused at the door and took a minute to run her fingers through her hair. Taking a deep breath, she opened it. There he stood, smiling.

"Good evening, doctor," she said in a husky voice that caused his body to tighten uncomfortably. "Come on in. We're not ready yet."

They stood underneath the entranceway chandelier facing each other. Caleb's appreciative eyes roamed her entire body, taking in all of her features. She tried not to blush under the intensity of his stare.

Caleb had known since their first date that Miranda had excellent fashion sense, and so he'd spent time on the drive over bracing himself for something nice. And the sight of her in the black dress didn't disappoint.

The material draped over her arms and shoulders, crisscrossing at her breasts and leaving him with the tantalizing smooth skin, tempting collarbones and slender neck.

Her eyes met his and he grinned. She blushed and glanced down. Sensual and confident one second, shy the next. Caleb would never understand her.

"I know you've changed a lot since we were together, but I'm still holding out that some of your favorites haven't." With that, Caleb moved his left hand from behind his back and presented Miranda with a single perfect lily.

There were times when her eyes would darken to jet-black, and if possible make her even more beautiful. And one of those times had to be then. Her lips curved upward and Caleb fought the insane urge to reach down and kiss her until they were both gasping for air.

"Thank you," she said softly. "I'd forgotten how incredibly romantic you could be."

"Here's to remembering good memories and making better ones." He took a step forward and gently kissed her on her cheek. "Now, if I wasn't mistaken, I get to have two beautiful women on my arm tonight."

"Kiss my sister again and you might not have an arm, Blackfox."

Caleb looked over Miranda's shoulder to see Darren making slow progress down the hallway.

"Looks like those therapy sessions must be working out for you, man. How about we increase them to three days a week?" he suggested with a straight face, although he knew that no one in their right mind would agree to the intensive treatments. The quick look of haunting fear that crossed Darren's face sparked a hint of glee in Caleb.

"Nothing's worth that amount of grief," Darren replied. "Even if it meant I'd never see your face again."

Miranda turned and opened her lips to respond,

but Caleb moved to touch her hand. She had always been the peacemaker between them and as much as he appreciated her defense of him in the past, Miranda's overprotectiveness had only served to increase the animosity between himself and her older brother.

"Sweetheart, why don't you go put the flower in water?" he said. In a softer voice, he continued, "I can handle the big bad brother."

Miranda leaned into him. The intoxicating scent of her perfume mixed with her own sweet fragrance floated up to his nostrils.

"But can you handle the big bad little sister?" She winked and then strolled down the hallway. He watched her smooth and graceful movements until she disappeared from view. Shaking his head and feeling a rush of carefree happiness that he hadn't felt in too long, Caleb turned his attention to his current unwilling patient.

"Man, Darren, where is the love? I pulled strings to get you one of the best physical therapists at the hospital, not to mention the prettiest, and you can't ease up a little on the animosity?" He held up his right hand, showing his thumb and index finger close together. "Just a tiny bit?" Caleb grinned wider, making a show for Miranda who had just returned.

Darren's eyes narrowed and it looked to Caleb as if he wanted to use the crutch as a baseball bat against his head. Just in time, the sound of shoes coming down the steps redirected all of their attention.

"Sorry I took so long."

Caleb moved to stand close to Kelly. With his hand out, he smiled. "Beauty is always worth the wait. And I get to be the envy of my brothers since I have two on my arms tonight."

"You've got brothers?" Kelly asked.

"One older and one younger. I've also got a little sister. You remind me of her."

"Is she smart?"

"Very, she's also stubborn and hardheaded. Once, when my parents had to go out to a company party, she took my brother's Porsche and raced it at the old motor speedway."

Kelly's eyes were as wide as her disbelieving mouth. "She stole a Porsche?"

"Yep, thing is we never would have known if she hadn't won and gotten her picture in the paper," Caleb said, laughing.

"Did she go to jail?"

"Worse." He grinned broadly.

"Did they lock her in her room with no TV and take away her phone?"

"Well, the story goes that it took my dad a week to figure out the best punishment. At that time Regan only liked to race cars, she hated getting dirty fixing them. So, her punishment was that every day after school and on weekends, she had to work at the dealership or work on restoring Dad's old cars."

"That doesn't seem that bad."

"Oh, did I forget to mention she got her license taken away for a year? Regan had to beg my younger brother to drive her everywhere."

"Not good," Kelly said. She looked down at her book bag as she contemplated what Caleb had said.

Caleb glanced at Miranda. Her expression was soft and contemplative while her lips curved into a half smile. Emotion squeezed his throat. He wanted that look. No, Caleb realized in an instant. He needed that look. And if there was one thing that he could do best it was get what he needed. Turning up the charm, he grinned at Miranda and Kelly. "All right, ladies, I've got a houseful of people eager to feed you wonderful food and stories. So shall we get on the road?"

"Make sure you drive safely, Blackfox," Darren ordered.

"Are you sure you don't want to come with us?" Miranda asked.

"Positive. I've got some work to do and when I finish, I'm going to sit on the couch and catch up on my Tivo. Honest to God, I'm glad you're leaving. There's too much estrogen in this house for a man to take."

Miranda walked over to her brother and gave him a peck on the cheek. "Call me if you need anything."

"Just have some fun."

She walked back into the foyer and stopped as her eyes landed on Caleb and he let out an appreciate whistle. "You look good enough to eat, Miranda."

"Thank you." She smoothed down the front of her formfitting black dress that ended right above her knees. "You look very handsome tonight, as well."

That was an understatement. As her girlfriends would say, the man was *fine*. Caleb didn't just wear the dark gray pleated slacks, turtleneck and tweed jacket. He made it look good. His sharp chin, strong jaw and deep warm brown eyes could have landed him on a fashion runway while his full kissable lips made him the perfect poster boy for lip balm.

"I'm ready," Kelly announced. Miranda turned and watched the child dragging her stuffed backpack.

"Are you sure she doesn't need a sleeping bag?" Miranda asked Caleb.

"Positive. Everything will be provided. Including the all-you-can-eat cookies and ice cream."

"Yippee. Can we leave now?" Kelly pushed.

Miranda nodded. "I just need to get my purse and coat."

Chapter 17

After they pulled out of the driveway, Miranda turned toward Caleb and asked, "How did I let you talk me into this?"

"You lost a bet and it was either meet the family or strip naked and give me your panties."

"Shh," she hissed darting a quick look in the backseat.

"Kelly is too busy playing video games and, trust me, you could scream at the top of your lungs and she couldn't hear you through the headphones."

Miranda's lips curved up even as she tried to stop them. "I think she really likes you."

"No." Caleb chuckled. "I think she really likes the car. It tends to have that kind of affect on kids." Caleb glanced in the rearview mirror and watched Kelly as her mouth twisted in concentration. Not one to play video games, he'd never taken advantage of the built-in Sony PlayStation or the DVD player that had come pre-installed with the SUV.

"She thought you were cool before the car." Miranda laughed, and then a shadow crossed her face. "I wonder if it's too soon."

"Too soon?"

"Do you want me to leave my brother alone all night?"

"As his doctor I can sign off that he'll be fine."

"I always thought of Darren as my invincible older brother. Since the accident he's been very vulnerable."

Vulnerable? Darren Tyler? Caleb snorted inwardly. The man had given him his first black eye. The thought of Darren as being vulnerable made him laugh so hard that he almost ran over an orange cone. If only Miranda knew. "Trust me, Darren is many things, but he's not vulnerable."

"Quit it, Caleb. He actually likes you."

"Impossible."

"Apparently, he thinks we're good together."

"I should probably order another CAT scan for his brain. Maybe the accident crossed some wires." He laughed.

"He told me about Jessica Greene."

This time Caleb did swerve. "He told you that he set me up?"

"Yes."

"Well, I'll be damned."

"Or exonerated. I just jumped to the wrong conclusion and I didn't want to listen. I loved you so much…"

Her voice trailed, but she could tell from the warm expression that came over his face that he understood her meaning. "It's in the past, Miranda."

He reached out and took her hand within his own. "I just want to build on what we have now. You, me and Kelly."

She smiled and took it, content for the moment. All was right in her world.

The trip to his parents' house was accomplished in no time. As he drove through an open gate, Miranda couldn't help but marvel at the long tree-lined driveway. The large colonial house was something out of *Gone with the Wind*. Only a few other cars lined the drive as he parked. The lights were on all through the place and music trickled out from the back.

"Wow, is this place big," Kelly announced.

"No kidding," Miranda responded. "Just when I forget that you're a Blackfox, something happens to remind me that you still have the silver spoon."

"No. Now everyone in my family puts on their own clothes, flushes and wipes. If you're looking for the Rockefellers, Biltmores or Hiltons, this isn't the place. We're just like everyone else."

"With million-dollar estates, prize horses, car dealerships and a trucking conglomerate."

"Did I hear horses?"

Caleb leaned back and laughed as Kelly ripped off her wireless headphones in excitement. "We used to have horses in the stable. Once all of us left home, my parents decided to donate them to a local riding school that helps with at-risk teenagers."

Her face fell and Caleb quickly added, "My sister and her new husband have horses. I'm sure that they would love to have you over to the house to ride."

Her eyes were big as saucers. "Really?"

"Really. I'll introduce you to them tonight."

"Yeah!"

"So what exactly happens tonight?" Miranda asked.

"We eat, drink. You meet my family. Kelly will have a load of fun with the other kids, want to go home with my cousin's kids for a sleepover, you will act like the worried parent, but give in to her pleas."

"And then what?"

"You're coming home with me."

"And why would I want to do that?"

"Because I need you to sleep over in my bed tonight."

"I'm not going, Caleb."

"Kelly will have a great time and I'll have you home before lunch."

"I'm not coming home with you, Caleb."

"You sound like a broken record."

"Evidently you're not listening."

All day she had been repeating the words and all day he'd been wooing her. First, he'd sent her a large box of chocolates and flowers. Ever since he'd mentioned his grandparents' party, she'd been telling him that she and Kelly would not be going. Excuse after excuse had been offered, but he had negated them all with his charming persuasiveness.

During the mornings and afternoons, while Kelly was in school and Darren either at physical therapy or working in Dad's old office, she'd caught up on her work reports, finished filling out information for her taxes, cleaned the house and started to get back into her old hobby of sewing.

She was grateful for the distractions. Were it not for the little things to occupy her mind, she would have had to deal with her conflicting feelings toward Caleb.

He called her several times a day, and it bothered her to realize that she began to look forward to those conversations. For the past few weeks she'd gotten used to him continually popping by the house on one pretext or another. He had dinner with them every night. It had almost become a matter of form.

One night, after Miranda had accidentally managed to burn the meat loaf, Caleb had arrived at the front door with Chinese takeout. One evening they grilled salmon on her father's gas grill. Another night they all had hamburgers and French fries in the living room while watching a movie.

With her older brother and Kelly as chaperones, they somehow managed to keep their hands off one another. Yet each time she caught him watching her, the smoldering flame of desire in his eyes was all too evident and it never failed to kindle a response in her.

Only when Caleb kissed her good night did Miranda catch a glimpse of the hunger he kept in check. Each time he kissed her with such urgency that he'd left her breathless with wanting.

Pushing away the lingering memory of his lips pressed against hers and his fingertips brushing against her breasts, Miranda followed Kelly and Caleb into the mansion.

As they entered the foyer, Caleb stepped behind Miranda to remove her coat.

Contrary to the outside appearance, the interior of the house held a distinctly eclectic blend of African-American artwork and contemporary interior design. The gleaming wood floors were subtly enhanced with a plush handwoven rug. She wanted to take off her shoes and curl her toes in its softness. Paintings graced the cream-colored walls, softly backlit with track lighting. The scent of home cooking blended with the faint musk of incense and jasmine.

"Let me take your coat," Caleb said.

Miranda turned politely and, as his fingers touched her shoulders, she inhaled the scent of his cologne mingled with the heavy smell of bread, leaving her hungry. Lifting the coat from her shoulders, he murmured only loud enough for her to hear. "You're running out of time, Miranda. One way or another you're going to be in my bed."

The living room opened to the dining room that was more family-oriented than formal. A table of the deepest mahogany wood was loaded with platters and serving trays of food.

The chairs looked as if they had been crafted by hand with intricate circle designs and comfortable cushions. Miranda imagined large Thanksgiving dinners and Blackfox women sitting, holding their cards, while gossiping over who played the best game of bridge.

Before she could orient herself, a group of teens converged upon them.

"Hi, I'm Corinne and this is my sister, Bethany. We're here to bring Kelly to the secret slumber party."

"Secret, huh?" Miranda smiled.

"Don't worry, they're going to be under the strict supervision of my younger cousin."

"All right, then. Come give me a hug and a kiss."

Kelly ran over and hugged her legs as Miranda bent over and kissed her on the top of her hair.

"Be good and have fun."

"No problem."

She watched the girls run off and then returned her attention to the man standing at her side.

"She's growing up way too fast. Pretty soon she'll be a teenager."

"Don't rush it. You've got time."

Suddenly well aware of how untrue his statement was, Miranda was hit with a wave of guilt. Caleb really adored the little girl and her leaving would hurt him just as much as it would her.

"Where have you been? You're late," a voice interrupted her thoughts.

"Well, nice to see you too, Savannah." Caleb hugged the pregnant woman.

"And this gorgeous woman who must have taken pity on you must be Miranda."

Miranda took the woman's open hand and shook it. "I've heard a lot of good things about you, Savannah."

"Don't believe a word he says," she replied.

Miranda giggled at the hurt look on Caleb's face. "My daughter, Kelly, is a student at your middle school."

"Wonderful. We can talk all about it. First you must come with me. We need your expertise in the kitchen."

Leaving Caleb with a puzzled look on his face, Miranda waved goodbye and allowed Savannah to lead her to the kitchen. Caleb wasn't the only one confused. Savannah mentioned needing her cooking skills. What cooking skills? The pregnant woman was either delusional or insane.

Inside the kitchen all the women were gathered around the table sipping Chardonnay. Savannah made the introductions and the gossip continued. Before Miranda could take a seat at the table, a glass of wine materialized and she was pulled into the conversation.

Minutes later, Caleb strolled in and smiled as he saw all of them sitting around the table with guilty expressions on their faces.

"Well, well, well, looks kinda cozy up in here. And I thought y'all would be cooking up a storm. You got some hungry men waiting outside."

Rolling up her dish towel, Caleb's mother gave

her son a good whack on the rear end. "Out...
Out. You're disturbing our work. Go tell those
cigar-smoking, beer-drinking male relatives of
yours that dinner will be served when the women
feel like it."

Laughing, Caleb ducked out of the kitchen pro-
testing that women had invaded his home.

As soon as he left, their little group got to work
taking covered dishes out of the oven and fridge.

As everyone sat down at the dinner table, the
war between the sexes began. Of course Caleb's
little brother had to be leading the men into battle.

"This food should definitely be out-of-sight...
all you beautiful women in one kitchen. Then
again I've never known you to cook, Savannah.
So that goes to prove you're in love," Trey teased.

"Well, dear cousin—" Savannah cocked her
head to the side "—if you'd spent more time at
home than on the football field chasing cheerleaders, you might have learned a thing or two."

Groans from the men drowned out the wom-
en's laughter at Savannah's quick comeback.

Sasha, Trey's fiancée, arched a well-tended
eyebrow. "Chasing cheerleaders? And here I
thought that you were the studious type."

"Come on, Sasha, I had to chase something
since I hadn't met you yet," Trey replied.

His response earned him major points for
flattery. Miranda watched as he leaned over and

placed a kiss on Sasha's cheek. Predictably, the women melted. Point for the men.

Chuckling, James, the bachelor-uncle Caleb had introduced her to before sitting down at the table, attempted to bring his comrades back from the edge by invoking single-male solidarity.

"Pull up, Trey. My man, you are in serious danger of losing your player's card."

As all of them, even the married ones, jumped on the bandwagon proclaiming the virtues of brotherhood, dating, boys' night out and clubbing, the women began to plan an all-out war. Silently communicating, using the ancient signal of rolling their eyes, they prepared. The invocation of player's card was the men's first, last and biggest mistake. It was time to bring them to their knees.

Caleb, a sometime participant and otherwise silent observer, leaned toward Miranda chuckling and whispered, "Be gentle, for they know not what they do."

She smiled a frosty grin and lifted her wineglass to signal the charge. "Ladies, can you believe this? Here I was thinking we'd be having dinner with men tonight. From the conversation I'm hearing it looks like only boys came to this table."

Regan, Caleb's sister, continued. "Hmm...girl, you're right. Boys who want to play with cards and talk about being bachelors."

Caleb's aunt Brenda laid down the trump card like a sista playing spades.

"Oh, and George," she said coolly. "You can keep your player's card and I hope it keeps you company tonight because this woman needs a man, not a boy." That comment led to a crushing defeat. Raising their hands and throwing out their imaginary player's cards, the men offered their unconditional surrender.

The rest of dinner was filled with women swapping stories, gossip, dating advice and beauty secrets while the men talked sports teams, stock options and 401K. After the meal was finished and dessert consumed, everyone helped to clear away the dishes and the music was turned on.

Relinquishing her glass of wine, Miranda allowed Caleb's father to lead her into the living room and join the other couples on the impromptu dance floor. Their dance was interrupted when Miranda had to take a phone call. After the call, she reclaimed her glass and took a seat on the sofa. Closing her eyes, Miranda savored the dry warmth of the wine as it trickled down her throat and relaxed at the sound of Luther Vandross telling her what love was all about.

Minutes later, she heard his voice. "I hope you're not falling asleep yet."

Startled, she opened her eyes to see Caleb seated comfortably next to her. "No. I'm just enjoying the music."

Smiling, he stood up and reached out his hand. "Good. I've waited all night for a dance."

She placed her hand in his and followed him out onto the floor. Curling her arms around his neck, she sighed and laid her head upon his chest. Miranda could feel the strength in his arms as they slowly encircled her waist and rested lightly upon the middle of her back. He touched her as if she was too fragile to be held tightly and too precious to let go. In that manner, they danced or swayed to the music.

They say that people are born to conform to culture. However, there are many things that go beyond culture—race, language and ethnicity— to encompass basic human nature. One of those fundamental things is the need to touch and the need to be touched, connect with another person by physical contact. Tonight, her skin rejoiced in the feeling of being touched; and the warmth of being held filled her soul.

"You're not falling asleep on me are you?" Caleb whispered.

She raised her head from its nice spot on his chest and replied, "No."

"Good." He grinned broadly. "I'll take you home."

* * *

Minutes later, when Caleb pulled to a stop in his driveway, Miranda barely managed to hide her smile. "I thought you were taking me home."

His gaze never wavered. "My home, for now. One day it might be our home."

Her heart skipped a beat. It wasn't as if he hadn't talked about getting married when they'd first met. In their ideal futures, Caleb would have continued to practice medicine and Miranda would have been a working mother to a tribe of Daddy's little girls. Shaking off the memories, she removed her seat belt.

"So I guess we're having our own little slumber party, after all?"

"I can make a tent out of my sheets if you really want to have a little campout."

"I always like the outdoors," Miranda said as she entered the house via the garage doors. "But I like indoor bathrooms a lot better."

"Good. How about I show you to your bathroom while I slip into something more comfortable."

Miranda laughed at the devilish expression on his face. "Isn't that something the seducing woman would say?"

"Work with me, sweetheart. I've been thinking of how to get you back in my bed since I woke up alone Wednesday morning."

"You could have asked."

"Too easy."

He led her up the stairs. "I'll be right down the hall if you need me."

She crossed through the guest bedroom and into the bathroom. The light stone-colored room with sand-colored inscribed tiles was a woman's dream. The frosted windows and recessed lighting softened the room and warmed the hardwood floor.

A large marble sink stood by itself next to a white painted wood vanity tower. The glass-framed shower stood separated from the bath. Miranda had only seen bathtubs like that one in movies or in designer magazines. Its deep polished inside spoke of long soaks with low lights and burning candles.

She smiled seeing herself with a green oatmeal avocado facemask and hair covered by a towel, sitting in the tub with her eyes closed. In the silence of the house, Miranda heard what sounded like singing. Curious, she went back out in the hallway and walked toward the master bedroom.

As Miranda stepped into Caleb's domain, her jaw dropped.

"I'll make love to you…"

The deep voice, as rich as dark chocolate, was raised in song. Miranda nearly laughed aloud.

Caleb was singing!

Caleb was singing in the shower.

The man who lip-synced at church was singing.

Caught in a snare of compulsion, she reached out and carefully pushed the door open a few more inches. Now she could see the shower stall. The glass was only slightly filmed with soap and water. She could not attribute all of the moisture on her skin to the steam that filled the small room. Nor could the steam account for her rapid breathing and a tingling in her breasts as her nipples tightened.

Maybe he heard the creak of the door opening or maybe he sensed her presence, but the water stopped.

"Did you enjoy the show?" he asked. After drying himself off, he exited the shower stall with only a short towel wrapped low on his hips.

Toying with the hem of her skirt, Miranda unabashedly watched as he swaggered toward her. "Very much. I didn't know you could sing."

"Only in the shower."

"I'd love to get a private serenade," she said in a sultry tone.

His lips brushed hers, gently teasing the edges of her mouth until she opened and kissed him back. The urgency of why she'd wanted to speak with him slipped from her thoughts, replaced by the heat of his kiss.

"I want you," he murmured into her mouth, his tongue flickering against her lips. Miranda moaned and sucked his bottom lip, pressing her body against his.

"Same here," she whispered just before she deepened the kiss, tasting his mouth, caressing his tongue.

"I've been waiting all night to get you out of that dress," he groaned, pulling her hips tight against his. Through the cotton towel, Miranda had no doubt that he was as aroused as she was. But even though she was practically attacking him, he wanted to be certain she was ready.

She anchored her hands on his bare shoulders and stood on her tiptoes. Getting as close to his ear as possible, she nipped the lobe, and traced the edge with her tongue. "You're not the only one who's been thinking about getting naked."

He moved to suckle her neck and squeeze her rear. Miranda's knees buckled, leaving her clutching his shoulders. Her head spun with the scent, the taste and the feel of him against her. Her hands skimmed down his sides, sculpting the smooth torso and stomach.

Once in the bedroom, Miranda didn't know who moved first or how it happened but before she could say anything else, he'd slid the straps off her shoulders, and the dress fell, pooling at her feet. Self-conscious, Miranda moved to slide under the covers, but Caleb stopped her and sat down on the bed. She resolutely kept her eyes on his. He slid his hands down her arms, from shoulder to wrists. And then he laid her back carefully and let his eyes roam over her as she had done to him earlier in the evening. The weight of his regard was enough to make her nipples contract and her whole body tense.

His hands soon followed the path his eyes had scored. His fingertips started at her ankles and then he ran them slowly up her body, stroking and teasing the skin as he went. Miranda was writhing by the time he'd made it up to her thighs and completely breathless when his fingertips captured her breasts.

Her eyes traveled over the planes of his face and the perfect curve of his lips, down to the hard muscles of his shoulders and chest to his stomach and the faint line of hair that she'd always found fascinating. Some women loved shoulders, muscled arms or bottoms. But Miranda had always loved Caleb's chest. She loved his clean, hairless and perfectly sculpted chest with toned muscles and long waist. His body was wonderful, like a fantasy come to life. His sex was equally as impressive.

Yet it was only the space of one breath to the next when he'd move to position himself on top of her. Everything seemed to tighten as her flesh came into contact with his. Caleb was so hot. He was like a flame and she wanted to burn beside him.

"I will love you with every breath I take," he vowed. "And kiss you—" his fingers unclasped her bra "—lovingly—" they moved to her back and easily undid her bra strap "—slowly—" they moved forward to cup her breasts, thumbs gently kneading the flesh "—over every inch of your skin."

She fought to clear her head, but then his lips claimed hers in a kiss that burned all the way to her toes. "You are so beautiful, sweetheart."

Then he dropped his head and began to kiss, nip and suck on her neck. She felt the heat of his hands on her breasts. "So soft, so perfect."

He rested his weight on his knees and lowered his head. Her body quivered as his lips kissed a hot path down her collarbone toward her breasts. His mouth was hot and demanding, sucking and nuzzling with passionate urgency. When he took the tip of her breast between his teeth every muscle in her body tensed and Miranda forgot to breathe. She clutched his shoulders and rubbed the ridges along his spine. He worked one hand between her thighs and found her damp and ready. Caleb peeled off her silk panties. She spread her legs. He blew gently, stirring the silky dark hair with his breath. He used his fingers and tongue to bring her to the edge of climax, slowly, teasingly, until she was writhing and clawing at him.

"Caleb! I need you now!" she panted, waves of electric current rolling down her spine.

"Not yet," he said moving upward to suckle her breast while sliding a finger deep into her, pressing the sensitive nub with his thumb.

Her orgasm exploded through her causing her back to arch, her heels drummed on the mattress, her fingers clutched his shoulders for purchase as a hoarse cry escaped her throat. The initial shockwave passed, but Caleb fastened his mouth on the sensitive curve of her neck and his finger pressed deeper relentlessly wringing a second orgasm from her. This time she shrieked, flinging an arm over her face to muffle her cries.

He moved to lie beside her. She could do little more than gasp and whimper for several minutes, but he did not seem rushed. He tenderly touched her face. It took several heartbeats for her mind to begin functioning. But as she looked down at Caleb's erection, Miranda realized that he was more concerned about her pleasure than his own, and would be satisfied even if they stopped now. When they'd been together in college, he had been a wonderful lover. He had never been selfishly concerned with his release, or determined to prove something. But this was different and she knew that this older, more mature Caleb had a depth of caring that she had never experienced before. She realized that her brother had been wrong. He was not merely attracted to her. Caleb loved her.

This realization brought tears to her eyes. Alarmed, he started to speak, but she silenced him with a finger pressed to his lips. He kissed the saltiness from her cheeks.

"You are incredible," she whispered.

"You are beautiful," he replied. "And you're mine."

She kissed him, a long sweet kiss, caressing his face. "Am I yours?"

"No doubt."

"Then you're mine, doctor." She rose up on one elbow and looked at him, so wonderfully featured and handsome.

She kissed him again, with more passion this time. The aftershocks of her two devastating climaxes had passed, and though she normally would have been exhausted, she was eager for more. When he tried to sit up, she pressed him down and began playfully trailing her hair across his body. She showered kisses on his chest, his thighs. He clenched his fists in the blankets when she reached his stiffness and felt him jump gently under her hands.

"I need to protect you," he gasped.

Well aware of what her hand was doing to him, Miranda's lips curved into a seductive smile. "As a doctor I'm sure you have something for emergency situations like this."

"Emergency?" he groaned hoarsely.

"Life-threatening crisis."

"Nightstand," he gasped as her hand caressed his manhood.

Miranda moved quickly to retrieve a condom. "Perfect." Biting her lower lip in concentration she returned her attention to the perfect male specimen lying in the middle of the bed. Mustering every bit of concentration, she leisurely rolled the condom down while watching the play of emotion cross his face. Once finished, she shifted her weight, kneeling over him, with her hands braced against his chest.

Almost without conscious thought, she lowered herself slowly onto him, feeling his hands on her hips, guiding her, supporting her as he penetrated her inch by glorious inch until he was fully inside. Everything in her body tensed and for several heartbeats, neither moved. And then the need for friction took control. Miranda rose and then dropped downward; bringing him home again in a quick thrust.

He was giving her so much pure pleasure, so many sensations that her mind gave up trying to analyze them. She was seared by the bruising heat of his hands where they gripped her hips. The fullness of her breasts, teased into hard-tipped peaks by his tongue and teeth. The trembling in her legs and arms as she supported her own weight. But most of all, the heated friction of him sliding within, building the tension until she thought she would scream from the bliss.

To stifle her cries, she bit him again and dug her fingernails into his arms. He raked his teeth gently nipping her shoulder, careful not to break the skin. He moved to meet her downward thrusts, nearly lifting her from the mattress as the pace of their coupling increased. His finger clenched on her hips, pulling her down as he thrust upward so strongly that she shattered, crying out his name as climax took over. A heartbeat later, after Caleb enjoyed his own release, Miranda collapsed against his chest. Her breath escaped her in a long shuddering sigh. They lay like that for some time. He cupped her face in his hands and kissed her. She murmured his name, pleasantly exhausted, happier than she had been in years. The warmth of his breath as well as that of his body comforted her.

Sometime later he made love to her again, starting slowly and building to a frenzy. He knelt on the bed and turned her around, entering her while she writhed on the pillows. Her need and want of him took over her senses. Their motion fell in sync and Miranda pushed backward determined to bring him deeper and deeper into her. With each stroke, her passion increased.

"Love you," she moaned as her entire body shook with pleasure. Her voice was hoarse with the sheer intensity of the sweet release. "Love you."

Between one breath and the next, she started to drift into slumber. Barely able to move after making love, he had shifted, making room for her to curve into the warmth of his body, his arms wrapped around her stomach.

"How about my birthday?" he asked lazily.

They were sprawled together on the bed, the pillows were scattered on the floor and the covers were tangled.

"Hmm?" she replied. Her mind struggled to answer his question as he nuzzled her shoulder and her body began to respond.

"Your brother should be recovered from his accident, Kelly will be out of school and it'll be plenty of time for your parents to fly back."

"Baby, what are you talking about?"

"Our wedding date."

Pulling away, Miranda prepared to slip out from under the covers when he caught her wrist. "It's really late, Caleb. I'd better get home."

"What just happened, Miranda? I just mentioned marriage and you're running away."

"We can't get married."

Frustrated with the turn of events, Caleb had to rein in the urge to shake the woman he loved. "Look, I know that your first marriage didn't turn out well but that doesn't mean that ours will be the same."

"I can't marry you."

"Why?"

She tugged her hand. "Don't ask, please. I just can't."

Her pleading eyes got to him. Not wanting to upset her even further, he reined in his growing annoyance. "Then you can at least spend the night here. I'll make an effort to stay on my side of the bed."

The sheet slipped from her chest and his eyes locked on to the sight of her erect nipples. His body reacted immediately and made a liar out of him. There was no way he'd stay on his side of the bed. He wanted her again, like a drug.

"I know that you'll keep your word, but I don't trust myself that much right now."

"Is that all?" he asked. His tone slightly guarded.

She smiled, leaned forward and kissed him. "Making love to you was… I can't describe it, but no matter how much I want to stay with you tonight, I don't want to rush this."

"I don't want to let you go."

"You could make this a little easier." She sighed.

He laughed at her sigh of regret. With a devilish grin, he gave her a hard kiss before he stood and sauntered naked into the bathroom.

Chapter 18

The clock on her nightstand read 3:47 a.m. With a sigh of impatience, Miranda got out of bed, pulled on her robe and headed to the kitchen. If she couldn't sleep then there was no use tossing and turning. And from her past experience, action was the best relief for insomnia.

After brewing a pot of coffee, she went into her father's office and shut the door behind her. Darren's blueprints and notes littered the desk and it took her a moment to clear off enough space for her notepad and coffee cup. It was the one room that she loved the most because she'd spent so much time in it as a child. An antique rolltop desk stood in the corner nestled between bookshelves and crammed with all of her father's favorite authors. Family photos and vacation pictures lined the walls, and her parents' wedding picture smiled at her from underneath the small brass reading lamp.

Shaking her head, she turned to the right, pulled out the chair and took a seat at the desk. Tonight, she was determined to find Lucas Blackfox. Caleb's great-uncle might never know it, but his location would be her gift to the man she loved.

Turning on the computer, she logged on using her Justice Department credentials to log onto the secured servers. Pulling up the list from the detective agencies, she added them to the lists of names generated from her earlier search. Using a precompiled cross-search program, which would query Social Security, census, state and national government and judicial records, she pushed the button and sat back. Hopefully as soon as it finished, her list would shorten to less than half a page. But then what? What if she found his uncle tonight? There was still the fact that she'd lied to him about her marriage and about Kelly. How would he ever trust her again?

Miranda sniffed as tears of self-pity pooled in her eyes.

"Burning the midnight oil?"

Startled, she looked up to see her brother enter the room. Darren deftly maneuvered to sit in one of the leather chairs across from the desk. "You're getting good at using those crutches."

He grimaced. "I don't have much of a choice. It's the only way I can get next to Grace. She's got the catch-me-if-you-can thing going on."

Miranda tried to laugh, but it came out as a hiccup and a tear rolled down her cheek.

"Does the fact that you're in here crying have to do with Blackfox?"

"Everything has to do with Caleb." Miranda told him about Caleb's search for his great-uncle and the fact that he wanted to marry her. "I really don't know what to do."

"What does your heart tell you?" Darren asked.

Miranda closed her eyes and shook her head. "I'd expect something like that from Aunt Pat or Mom. Not you."

"Think about it. The last time I gave you advice, I told you to use your head. I'm not going to make the same mistake twice, and I think you should do the same."

Miranda digested his words quietly. "I trust Caleb." Just saying the words made her heart lighter. "I love him and I know that he would never do anything to endanger Kelly. But I made a promise, Darren."

"And it's tearing you up inside. Why don't you

talk to Ryan? Get his permission to tell Blackfox the truth."

She shook her head. "I can't get in touch with him now that the trial's started. Not to mention, I don't know if Caleb will be able to forgive me for lying."

"He says he loves you, right?"

Miranda nodded her agreement. "But will he trust me after I tell him the truth?"

Darren's face and voice softened. "The way I see it you don't have much of a choice. As soon as the trial is over Ryan's going to come for his daughter. And unless you plan on being Houdini and disappearing off the planet, the truth will get out."

Miranda felt chilled, imagining Caleb finding out about the charade from someone else. "As soon as I find his uncle, I'll tell him."

Just then the computer beeped. Her search was complete.

As the sunlight began to creep through the blinds the next morning, she placed printouts in a manila folder, sat back and rubbed her dry eyes. She'd found his missing great-uncle, but she was sure that the results would be bittersweet.

"This is going to hurt his grandfather deeply," she whispered. Logging off the computer, she flexed her shoulders and rolled her head forward and backward to loosen the tight muscles in her neck. Her search had returned zero leads even after she'd tried numerous variations of the man's name; but in the end it hadn't been the name or the age characteristic. Miranda frowned at the file. She knew why the thousands of dollars Marius had spent on private investigators had not borne fruit.

None of the agents had taken into account cultural history of the time period during which Lucas Blackfox had run away from home. Flipping open the folder, she looked at the copy of Joshua Fox's driver's license. Her eyes skipped over his age, weight and eye color, and zeroed in on the most important data point: race. Joshua Lucas Fox was listed as Caucasian. Like others fleeing the pre-Civil Rights south, Caleb's great-uncle had chosen not only to change his name when settling in Philadelphia, he'd changed his color.

Miranda grabbed her empty coffee cup and padded into the kitchen. Looking at the digital clock above the stove, she estimated that she had a little over a half hour before Kelly awoke. Ignoring the twinge of pain in her back, she poured a cup of last night's coffee and stuck it in the microwave. She needed to talk to Caleb today.

Chapter 19

"I don't believe it," Caleb repeated for the third time since she'd stepped into his office and handed over the file on Joshua Fox.

Miranda battled her misgivings and wondered if she should have told him that day. Maybe she should have waited until tomorrow.

"Everything about him matches up with the information I received from your brother."

"No, I have no doubt that this is my great-uncle. It's just that I've had a hell of a day."

Instantly out of her seat, Miranda walked over and stood behind Caleb. She pulled back the neck of his shirt, and with her hands above the shirt line, positioned her thumbs. Starting at the bottom of his neck and gliding up gently, she applied a bit of pressure with both thumbs. Next, she slowly massaged her hands up and down his spine.

"That feels like heaven. Don't stop."

"I won't if you tell me what happened."

"We had a gunshot wound come into the emergency room this morning."

"A police officer?" she asked, surprised.

"No, teenager." Caleb closed his eyes. Just when he thought he'd grown halfway removed from the day-to-day medical cases, life threw him a curveball. "Accidentally shot in the leg by a seventeen-year-old friend playing with his father's handgun."

"Did he make it?"

Caleb had taken him straight into the operating room and worked alongside one of the surgeons. "He'll live, but there's a chance that we'll have to amputate his leg. Christ, Miranda. The boy's mother said he was an All-star baseball player and had a chance at an athletic scholarship."

"It's not your fault, Caleb. You can't save the world."

"Doesn't keep me from trying, does it?" he asked rhetorically. The combination of Miranda's scent, melodic voice and massage drained the tension out of his body.

"I know and that's what makes you who you are. And I am proud of you for it."

He reached up and covered her hand with his own. "Thank you, baby."

"So what happens now?" she asked.

Caleb frowned and then remembered the information about his great-uncle. "I have to tell Marius. This is his baby. I need to let him decide what to do."

"And if he makes the decision to let it be?"

Caleb shrugged. To keep secrets from his family went against everything he believed in. But this was bigger than his conscience. "Then my grandfather will live the rest of his days without knowing what became of his older brother."

She came around in front of him and Caleb reached up and pulled her down into his lap, and swooped down for a kiss that sent the blood flowing to his heart and south to his lower body as well. He wrapped his arms around her. "I don't know what I would do without you, Miranda."

"Look, Caleb. There's something I have to tell you."

He shook his head and kissed her again. He knew she was going to talk about leaving and he didn't want to hear it. Not right then.

"Sweetheart, whatever it is, why don't you tell me tonight after the movie?"

"The movie?"

"It's pizza night."

She blinked. "I forgot."

"I might be a little late. I'm going to drop by Marius's on the way over and give him the news."

She nodded slowly, and then leaned in to kiss him tenderly on the lips.

"I'll see you tonight."

He watched her backside as she exited the doorway and made a mental note. That evening he'd be making two stops. The first to deliver the file to his brother and the second would be to pick an engagement ring.

"I still wonder how Dad could give up his new toy for Africa," Miranda whispered in his ear.

Caleb looked away from the fifty-six-inch wall-mounted high-definition television and toward Miranda. He pulled her closer, and then released an extravagant sigh. "What men do for love."

"What women do for the men that they love," she countered.

"I would sacrifice."

"Sacrifice?"

"Being a doctor has taught me more about life than all the years of school. Before you came back into my life I only had two reasons to make any kind of sacrifice—work and family."

"And now?" Miranda whispered.

"I have three, you, my family and Kelly."

Her eyes dropped from his face and she leaned in close to rest her head against his chest. "I don't know what to say."

He rested his chin atop her head. "You don't have to say anything. I'm not the same man who needed constant reassurance and reaffirmation. I'm a man who loves you, Miranda Tyler. I'm a man who wants to protect and cherish you and your daughter for the rest of our lives. And I know that right now you're not ready to accept that yet. But I'm willing to wait."

Miranda pulled away and searched his face. Just as she was about to speak, the doorbell rang. Her brow creased. "Darren must have forgotten his keys."

Caleb shook his head as he tensed. "That's not Darren."

"How do you know?"

"I know."

"Is there something you want to tell me about?" Miranda's chin notched upward.

"Look, your brother's not coming home tonight."

"Oh." Her eyes widened. "But he's got a broken leg."

Caleb glanced over to the love seat and was relieved to see that Kelly continued to sleep. "You stay in here and I'll see who's at the door."

"All right."

He stood up and made his way to the front of the house. A quick look through the peephole confirmed it wasn't Darren or the neighbors. Caleb unlocked the door and swung it open. "Can I help you?"

"I'm here for Miranda and Kelly."

Caleb's eyes narrowed. The stranger was tall, bald and built like a football defensive tackle. Normally, when faced with a man about two times his body weight and muscle mass, he'd have been intimidated. However, courtesy of his medical training, he knew of a few ways to bring even the biggest man to his knees.

"And who are you?" Caleb demanded.

"Daddy!" Kelly screamed.

Caleb frowned as, out of nowhere, Kelly barreled past him and into the man's waiting arms.

"My baby. God, I've missed you."

Caleb's jaw tensed. So this was Miranda's ex-husband and Kelly's adopted father. He could have gone through life hating a faceless man, but now he had come face-to-face with the man who'd married his woman, the man she'd turned to as a substitute for him. He was the man whom Kelly thought of as her father.

Caleb's jaw clenched as jealousy ripped through his guts.

"Dad, you're really here..." Kelly repeated.

Caleb stared, unable to look away from the intimate scene. And as his brain caught up with observing the happy reunion, he couldn't help but notice Kelly's uncanny resemblance to the man.

"Ryan." Miranda's voice drifted over Caleb's shoulder. "This is an unexpected visit. Is everything okay?" Caleb turned his head to see her standing a few feet away.

"It will be," Ryan replied.

"Why don't you and Kelly catch up in the den?"

Without waiting for an answer, Kelly took his hand and began to tug him toward the room she'd just left. "Come on, Dad, that's a keyword for 'get out of the room so they can talk.'"

They were halfway down the hallway when Miranda's ex-husband stopped and turned toward Caleb. "Dr. Blackfox."

Caleb met the man's eyes and the gratitude he saw took him by surprise. "I appreciate what you've done."

Even before Ryan and Kelly were out of hearing range, Caleb focused on Miranda. "She's his daughter, isn't she?"

He knows.

Miranda had been dreading this moment from the day she'd sat across from Caleb in the hospital cafeteria and lied. She didn't want to lie anymore, but she didn't really have a choice. It wasn't that she didn't trust Caleb; she trusted him with her most precious possession—her heart. But she'd sworn to her friend and her boss that the only person she would tell the truth to about Kelly's origins would be her brother. She'd given her word and, no matter the cost, she would have to keep it.

"Is Kelly your ex-husband's biological child?" Caleb asked.

Her heart squeezed as a result of looking into his eyes mutely and seeing the hurt in their brown depths. She couldn't answer. Wanted to, but couldn't. The words stuck in her throat.

"She is my daughter." Ryan's booming voice filled the hallway.

Caleb's eyes blazed and his voice was harsh. "This doesn't involve you."

"Yes, it does. Miranda won't answer because she made a promise to me."

"Ryan." She shook her head. "I can handle this."

Ryan stepped past Miranda and stood in front of Caleb. "You've already handled more than enough. Miranda and I were never married. Kelly's mother passed away from cancer two years ago and I've been raising her alone ever since. The truth is that we worked together for the Witness Protection

Agency. I am…I was a Federal Marshal. Two months ago I got mixed up in an FBI sting on a Russian crime boss. Because I was an eyewitness, I had to go into protective custody until the trial. But before I agreed to do anything, I needed to know that my daughter was safe. At that same time Miranda had requested leave to help her brother. The director saw it as an opportunity and I saw it as a chance for Kelly to be safe and to have some normalcy."

Miranda watched Caleb's expression throughout Ryan's speech and the fleeting moment of hope crashed against the impassivity of his face. Tears began to pool behind her eyes, but she blinked to hide them. Clearing her throat, she faced Ryan. "I need to talk to Caleb alone, please."

Ryan nodded and she made sure that he was completely out of hearing distance before stating the obvious. "I lied to you, not Ryan. I didn't want to, but I gave my word."

Feeling like the bottom of her shoes, she swallowed back tears. She should turn around and face the repercussions of her actions, but she didn't want to look, *couldn't* look at Caleb's face for fear of what she would see in his eyes.

She heard the sound of his footfalls against the hardwood floor and inhaled the sandalwood of his cologne as he stood behind her.

And when he turned her around, Miranda still didn't lift her face to his. Only the slight pressure of his finger on her chin forced her to look upward. Her tongue darted out over her parched lips and she looked into Caleb's soft brown eyes.

"I know."

Her brow creased with confusion and she stared at him with amazement.

"You're staring," he told her.

"Why aren't you mad? Why are you still here? Why are you holding me?"

"Would it make you feel better if I were upset?"

She swallowed hard. "Yes."

Caleb reached out and ran his fingertips over her cheeks. "Then feel better. I'm angry because you think that the love I have for you is so fragile that something like this could break it."

She shook her head. "You hate liars."

"I hate liver, too." He grinned. "But I ate it when your mother put it on my plate. Miranda, what you've done to protect Kelly makes me love you more."

Just looking up at him made the place in the center of her heart feel warm. She felt as if she'd swallowed a glass of her father's best cognac. His face. Lord, there should be a commandment against the beauty of his smile. She would never tire of seeing the chocolate brown of his skin against the white of his teeth and his midnight-black eyebrows. Miranda had never forgotten his face. She would never forget his face. Sometime in the past two months of being with Caleb, she'd unconsciously resigned herself to losing him. But she would happily go back to being alone as long as she had the memories of their time together and the image of his smile.

A tear slipped down her cheek. "I thought…"

"That I would leave?"

She nodded.

He placed two of his fingers underneath her chin and tilted her face upward. "I'm not leaving you tonight, tomorrow, next week, ever. Without a doubt we're going to fight. My family will interfere and your brother will complain. But this time I'm not letting you go."

"I love you, Caleb Blackfox," she declared.

He grinned and held her a little tighter. "I know."

"What do you mean you know?" Her eyes sparkled.

"Remember the other night in the middle of my bed when your fingernails ripped up the sheets?"

"Shh." She blushed.

"You told me *and* the neighborhood raccoons."

"No, I wasn't that loud."

"Baby, you almost made me deaf."

She laughed and the sound made her feel a hundred times better. "Beast."

"Only with you."

He leaned down and took her mouth with his. Miranda could barely squelch a moan as her body temperature rocketed upward.

"Have you two made up yet?" Kelly's voice drifted down the hallway.

Miranda pulled back and giggled like a school-girl. "I think we have."

"Not yet," he contradicted. Caleb's gaze locked with Miranda's; his heartbeat somehow tripled. "I need a promise."

"Anything," Miranda confessed, her heart warmed with a ray of hope.

He reached into his pocket and pulled out the box. He pried open the black velvet box and revealed a silver band with a stunning solitaire diamond. "I took my mother, sister, grandmother, and Savannah to Atlanta and spent half a day searching for this ring. I wanted it to be perfect and a symbol of how I felt."

Tears welled up and rolled down Miranda's face. "It's gorgeous."

Caleb lowered to one knee. "Miranda Eliza-beth Tyler, will you do me the honor of becoming my wife?"

"Yes," she answered softly.

She watched mesmerized as he took her left hand and slowly slid the ring on her left finger.

"Miranda's getting married. Miranda's getting married," Kelly began to sing.

Caleb stood and kissed her on the cheek and sang, "Caleb's getting married."

"You do know how to make an impression on a girl."

"I'd planned to propose at the end of the movie, when you were in tears."

"How did you know that I would cry when Beauty and the Beast were reunited?"

"The same way I knew Darren wouldn't be home and Kelly would pretend to be asleep."

"My brother knew you were going to propose?"

He squeezed her tight and smiled down. "Love, he and I thought the same thing. About time."

Chapter 20

"I don't see what the big rush was all about," Darren groused, loosening his necktie and taking a seat at one of the empty banquet tables. Everyone had rushed to the dance floor to humiliate themselves with the electric slide. Although he wouldn't admit it to a soul, he would have enjoyed being out there alongside his family. Caleb had agreed to remove the cast from his leg a week ago, but he wouldn't be cleared for dancing for a least a month.

He took a sip of chilled champagne and sat back.

"My dad is dancing," Kelly announced pulling up a chair next to his. Her shoes had been tossed aside and the flower girl was sporting numerous holes in her white stockings.

"He's doing a good job."

"My dad is dancing with your mother," she said in a scandalized voice.

"You turned him down."

"I don't dance," Kelly replied primly while toying with her corsage.

"Not yet, but you will dance at my wedding."

"No, I won't."

Darren smirked. "Yes, you will unless you want me to tell your dad about our little bargain that you skipped out on."

"What?"

"Remember our deal? You get a nice Christmas present for breaking up Blackfox and my sister."

Her eyes doubled to the size of small saucers. "Oh, that deal. You wouldn't tell my dad…would you?"

"In a heartbeat."

"One dance."

He stuck out his hand. "Deal. Now go fetch my future wife."

"Boy, are you going to have problems." Kelly rolled her eyes upward before launching herself out of the chair.

Darren laughed and enjoyed the sight of his parents, but his gaze turned to the woman dancing

with his father. His woman; all he had to do was
lay down a little more loving and it would be impossible for her to turn down his marriage pro-
posal. His eyes drifted toward his little sister and
the smile on his lips didn't dim. And then the
couple broke away from the crowd and headed in
his direction. He'd only grudgingly admitted
Blackfox into the family. Now, he was fielding
consulting engagement requests from the man's
corporate office.

Caleb took a seat in the chair beside him and
his sister sat in the man's lap. Miranda glowed
like a lightbulb. "I still don't see why ya'll had to
rush. There's nothing wrong with having a long
engagement. Unless…"

"Unless what?" Miranda grinned.

Darren's eyes went from his sister's beaming
smile to her stomach. "Unless you had to get
married."

Caleb tore his gaze from his wife's tempting
neck and addressed Darren. "No, we didn't."
Then, angling his neck forward, he looked at
Miranda. "Did we?"

She laughed and leaned back into his chest.
"No. But I almost wish we had. I've lost count of
the number of times I've been asked by your family
and mine when we're going to have a baby."

Caleb grinned. "As your doctor and your

husband, I'll be more than happy to do whatever it takes to make it happen."

"Stop." Darren choked and set aside his champagne glass. "I don't want to hear any more. I'm too young and handsome to be an uncle."

"Don't worry. Caleb Junior will age you quickly."

The newly married couple broke into peels of laughter at the horrified look on Darren's face.

The nuptials had been held a mere two months after Caleb had proposed in her parents' foyer. They had been harried for months in which Miranda and Caleb had moved her personal things from D.C. to his house. They had decided to keep her condominium as a convenience for the times that she would have to go back to her home office or for him to attend medical conferences.

Although they'd planned to have a small ceremony with a few friends and immediate family, Caleb's grandparents wouldn't hear of it. In the end, they had taken their vows in the largest church in town and in front of what felt like half the state of Georgia. Afterward, everyone had been invited to the country club for dinner and reception.

Caleb held his bride close. He hadn't slept in forty-eight hours, and the sight of her gliding down the aisle clad in creamy silk almost brought

him to his knees. He had rid her hair of the dozens
of pens and now his fingers drifted up her neck
to play with one of the fat curls.

"I think it's way past time we made our exit,"
he murmured as he nibbled on her neck.

"The party's just getting started." Miranda
giggled.

"Not the one I made reservations for," he
drawled.

"You have another party?"

"Yes, we do. And I don't want to be late." He
kissed her soundly and Darren cleared his throat.

"Good Lord, just because you married my
sister doesn't mean you get to kiss her in front of
me."

"Good point, my new brother-in-law. Now,
turn around so that I can kiss your sister behind
your back like I did when we were in college."

Darren's eyes narrowed and Miranda stood up
and pulled Caleb with her. "I'm ready to go home
now."

They tried to leave at ten o'clock, but it was
well past midnight before Caleb carried his wife
over the threshold of their house. He didn't set her
feet down until he'd reached the bedroom. She
turned toward him and reached for the buttons of
his shirt. Her fingers trembled, but they worked

steadily. Moments later, she dropped it and his undershirt to the floor.

Caleb's long, lean fingers began to work on her dress. He leaned over and trailed kisses upon her neck. With his left hand, he slowly pulled down the zipper of her dress. Miranda stepped toward the bed and the silky material joined his clothes on the floor.

At the sight of the lacy lingerie, he made a mental note to send his mother three dozen bouquets for Mother's Day. He laid her down on the bed and braced himself above her.

He smoothed her hair back and said softly, "I am the luckiest man on the planet, Mrs. Blackfox." His kiss was tender and loving.

"Likewise, Mr. Blackfox."

"I don't know how I kept myself from throwing you on the corporate jet and eloping in Vegas."

"I wouldn't have put up a fight. In fact, I would have packed our bags."

"Now she tells me." Caleb leaned her back on the bed and leaned over and nuzzled his face in her chest and used his teeth to tug open the small bow nestled between her full breasts. In no time at all, his tongue grazed each bud. Then he suckled them, pulled them into his mouth and enjoyed their fullness as much as he treasured the moans from Miranda's lips.

Taking her time, Miranda rubbed the contours

of his chest. Then she leaned closer and her lips followed the same trail. The painful pulse in his pants shot from barely manageable to merciless; he fought with all that he had not to lay her on the bed and make his way inside. His hands soon moved from her back to her front, roamed across the plains of her belly and then slipped beneath her panties to explore the bountiful territory of downy soft curls.

Another moan escaped from her lips the moment his fingers entered her passage. He knew what he was doing and he did it well. Using his mouth and using his fingers, he stroked, circled and petted. And when she was ready and her hips lifted from the bed in polite invitation, Caleb removed her panties and flung them to the floor. In short work, his pants followed and he rejoined her on the bed. He stretched out over her once again and made his way south, leisurely. This was a night that he wanted them both to remember.

Every touch, delicate kiss and warm breath was like a beautifully read scripture of loving prayer. He kissed everything, making his way down to the valley of her thighs. His lips were loving. His tongue was skilled and hot.

"Caleb!" Miranda groaned at the unexpected feel of his mouth and tongue. The sharp pleasure would have sent her to the ceiling had it not been for Caleb's strong arms locked around her thighs.

Her breath seemed to stop in her chest and it was difficult to draw in her next breath as ripples of pure pleasure streamed through her veins and she splintered with shards of bliss.

She opened her eyes and stared into his and the smile on her lips was a reflection of her body.

"I love you," Caleb groaned. He sank deep inside her. Her legs wrapped around his waist and her arms clasped his neck. And she whispered in his ear all the things she felt for him. And he moved in and out of her with long, measured strokes.

His head lowered and he claimed her mouth. In and out, his tongue probed in sync with his hardness.

When her body tensed with release, she cried out in his mouth as they exploded together, blazing up like an inferno reaching to the stars, and consumed to ashes. She was floating, warmth flooding her body, and he was there with her. He was holding her tight, his breath hot against her skin, his moan low in her ear.

Spent, he closed his eyes and relished in the feeling of bliss. Life at the moment was all he'd ever dreamed. His great-uncle and extended family were rejoining the Blackfox fold. His grandfather had stopped threatening to get his shotgun whenever Savannah brought Jack to the family dinners. Regan, his little sister, was expecting her first child. Trey was engaged to Sasha, the feisty research specialist had won their parents' affection and turned their parents' house upside down when she brought her Persian cat up for the weekend.

Marius was his only reason to worry. His older brother's demeanor grew colder and colder, and he was spending more and more time at the office, most likely structuring new deals. Caleb made a mental note to talk to his father about it when he and Miranda returned from their honeymoon.

Minutes or hours later, Miranda shifted beneath him. "Am I too heavy?" he asked, opening his eyes.

"If I say yes, will you hold it against me?" she teased.

"Want me to hold it against you?"

"I'd rather you kept it inside of me." She chuckled.

He rolled her over and she snuggled up against him. "Would you?" he growled with a mock ferocity against the top of her head.

"Oh, yes…"

"And what do I get, wife?"

"You get a son with your eyes."

"What if I want a daughter with your smile?" He looked down into her upturned face.

"Boys are easier," she replied.

Caleb thought about the misadventure and headaches Regan had put his parents through and sighed inwardly. If he couldn't say no to his wife—he'd never be able to deny his baby girl. He looked down into her heavy-lidded eyes.

"We'll see love…we'll see."

Torn between her past and present...

After Dark

DONNA HILL

ESSENCE BESTSELLING AUTHOR

Elizabeth swore off men after her husband left her for a younger woman...until sexy contractor Ron Powers charmed his way into her life. But just as Elizabeth is embarking on a journey of sensual self-discovery with Ron, her ex tells her he wants her back. And with Ron's radical past threatening their future, she's not sure what to do! So she turns to her "girlz"—Stephanie, Barbara, Anne Marie and Terri—for advice.

Pause for Men: Five fabulously fortysomething divas rewrite the book on romance.

Available the first week of July, wherever books are sold.

KIMANI
ROMANCE

Can she surrender to love?

WORKING MAN

Favorite Arabesque author

MELANIE SCHUSTER

Funny and feisty Dakota Phillips has almost everything
she wants. But her insecurities and independence have
kept her from searching for the perfect man. Then
she meets Nick—a self-made, take-charge mogul who
makes Dakota feel beautiful, desirable and maybe a
little too vulnerable. Dakota could easily move on...
except for a little complication called love.

*Available the first week of July,
wherever books are sold.*

KIMANI™
ROMANCE

www.kimanipress.com

KPMS0250707

Forgiveness takes courage...

A MEASURE OF
Faith

MAXINE BILLINGS

With her loving husband, a beautiful home and two
wonderful children, Lynnette Montgomery feels very
blessed. But a sudden car accident starts a chain of
events that tests her faith, and pulls to the forefront
memories of a very painful childhood. At forty years of
age, Lynnette comes to see that it takes a measure of
faith to help one through the pains of life.

"An enlightening read with an endearing family theme."
—*Romantic Times BOOKreviews*
on *The Breaking Point*

Available the first week of July
wherever books are sold.

www.kimanipress.com   KPMBNS0720707